UNTIL SHADOWS
FLEE AWAY

A COUNTRY DOCTOR'S STORY OF CHRISTMAS SEASONS PAST

CARL MATLOCK MD

Published in the United States by Matlock Publishing

ISBN: 978-0-9600521-5-8 Paperback

ISBN: 978-0-9600521-6-5 Ebook

Cover and Interior Design by Carl Matlock

Editing by Christy Distler, Avodah Editorial Services

Cover Images by shutterstock.com

First Edition

✿ Created with Vellum

Dedication

This book is dedicated to my wife, Janet Matlock. Her encouragement and assistance with initial
editing and story-line development has made the Country Doctor series possible and enjoyable for me to write.
She is still my inspiration after forty-nine years of marriage.

ACKNOWLEDGMENTS

I wish to thank Avodah Editorial Services and Christy Distler for the wonderful work of editing yet another one of my books. This is the third manuscript she has patiently edited for me.

PREFACE

This is a work of fiction, of tragedy and triumph in the lives of people, based on forty-seven years of both family and emergency medicine practice. The characters, except for my wife and family, are composites of the many patients, medical staff, and friends I encountered over those years. The story is based on real events and medical emergencies that occurred, but no living person is represented in the story-line. Instead, hundreds of patients and events are distilled into the main characters in this work.

Finally, the treatments described were those of the 1970s and in no way are they to be construed as recommendations for current treatment of any condition. Medicine has changed during my lifetime in astounding ways. Beginning with paper charts, a stethoscope, a primitive electrocardiographic machine, and simple tools of the trade, I began solo practice in a small town in Indiana. By the time I retired, I had advanced to an electronic stethoscope, computerized medical records, state-of-the-art electrocardiographic recording, and remote viewing of x-rays, ultra-sounds, CT scans, and MRIs.

The real satisfaction for me, however, has always been in caring for many wonderful and unforgettable people with the assistance of outstanding medical staff, both in my office and in the hospital setting.

My hope is that you enjoy the recounting of a simpler, and to my way of thinking, a friendlier time in the practice of medicine.

CHAPTER 1

The August sun beat down mercilessly and sweat trickled from my forehead as I entered my office in Glen Oaks through the back door. The ladies were already there ahead of me, busy in the spacious room that served as a combination lab and break area.

"Good morning, Donna. How are you this morning?"

"Fine, Doc. I hope you have your running shoes on. We have a busy day scheduled. Several new OB patients to be seen and two post-partum visits with their new babies. I'll have the first two ready in about five minutes." She opened the door to the front office and hurried out to retrieve another patient from the waiting room.

Glancing right, I nodded at Christine, my efficient office receptionist and assistant. She finished pouring the water into our brand-new coffee maker and turned, smiling. The aroma of fresh-brewed Folgers permeated the room as the carafe filled with the wonderful medium-blend coffee, evanescent bubbles floating on the surface of the magical liquid as it accumulated.

I threw my head back and inhaled deeply. "That smells heavenly."

"You're going to need it today." She smiled ingratiatingly. "Lucky you have such a great nurse in Donna, not to mention your marvelous receptionist and gourmet coffee maker, little old me." Christine curtsied with a flourish, then hurried to the outer front office to resume greeting and signing patients in for the morning.

I stretched and yawned to shake off the fatigue while waiting for the coffee to finish. My day had started at 5:30 with a hot breakfast prepared by my wife, Janet. Following that, I drove about fifteen miles through the country to begin rounds at the hospital in Glen Falls at 7:00, finishing just in time to get to the office at 9:00.

I relaxed at the break room table, sipping the scalding coffee, savoring every swallow and trusting it would revive me after another too-short night with less than six hours of sleep. An emergency surgery for a bowel obstruction in one of my elderly patients had kept me at the hospital until nearly midnight assisting Rob Hendrick, our general surgeon. The surgery had successfully relieved the obstruction, and Mr. Gooding spent the night in the ICU.

Donna opened the door and smiled. "First two are ready whenever you are. Christine has the OB revisits scheduled first, so they should go quickly."

The day proceeded normally until we were down to the last patient of the morning. Walking toward room 3, I noticed the troubled look on Donna's face as she handed me the chart.

"Something wrong?"

"This is a sad situation. Katherine Harrison is here with her parents, Bonita and Clayton Harrison. They are barely civil with Katy. The tension in the room is thick enough to cut with a knife."

"Is Katy pregnant?"

"Unfortunately, yes. I wouldn't want to be the young man responsible, even though it apparently was consensual. I'm sure they didn't stop to consider the possible consequences."

I shook my head. Pretty sixteen-year-old Katy Harrison. Deep-blue eyes, dark-brown hair, lovely olive complexion, vivacious, popular cheerleader, and excellent student at Glen Oaks High where she was a junior. Pregnant!

"Do you want me to come in with you? The room is already crowded, but Mr. Harrison looks like he is ready to explode. I feel sorry for all of them."

I grasped the doorknob. "Sure. Let's both go in and talk with them

6

first of all. Maybe you can comfort Katy while I deal with the situation."

Donna moved to the examination table where Katy sat slumped over, sobbing softly. She took her hand and offered a tissue to blot the tears and mascara running down her cheeks.

I pulled up a chair by Clayton and sat quietly for several moments, allowing him to compose himself. He stared at the floor, fists clenched, mouth clamped shut, and face stiff and frowning. Bonita sat beside him wiping tears, a strained expression on her face.

I cleared my throat. "Well, Katy, I take it that you believe you're pregnant. Do you know the date of your last menstrual period?"

Clayton growled. "She's pregnant all right. Been wearing tight jeans and clothes to hide it. I swear I'll kill that no-account Robert Mills."

Bonita laid her hand on his forearm. "Now, Clayton. Your going to jail won't solve anything and you know it. After all, Katy isn't exactly an innocent bystander."

I decided to try again. "Folks, it seems that none of you want this situation, not even Katy, but it's what we have to deal with. For her sake, let's all try to be objective. Teenage pregnancy is high risk, and I know that you want the best for her. Let's start at the beginning, one thing at a time." I nodded at Katy. "Are you able to recall the date of your last period?"

Katy dried her tears and blew her nose as Donna stroked her back. Then, in a barely audible voice, she answered hesitantly, "Four months ago. I ... I ... I've been feeling the baby move for a week."

"How long have you been intimate with Robert?"

Gaining courage, she looked up. "Only the last four months. Just twice. It must have happened the first time."

Bonita sighed. "We tried to teach her better than that. Honestly, I don't know what she was thinking. She was never self-destructive in the past. We had big plans for her: college, a career, an *educated* husband."

Defiantly looking away from her parents, Katy answered, "They were your plans, Mom. Yours and Dad's. They were never mine. Robert and I love each other. He plans to come over tonight and ask for your permission to marry me. Maybe you prefer the humiliation of me being a single mom? No, you don't want to be the ones disgraced by having an unwed, pregnant daughter. I didn't plan for this to happen, but now that it has, I want this baby, and I want to be married to the baby's father." She folded her arms across her chest and sat up straight for the first time.

Her last statement sucked all the air out of the room. Clayton relaxed a little and threw his head back, resting it against the wall. Bonita looked pained, but took Clayton's hand, gripping it tightly.

"Katy, you're right," she said. "We have been planning your life for you. Maybe it was wrong of us, but we did it because we love you so much. We just want the best for you." She wiped tears away with the tissue Donna handed her. "And now we want the best for this baby, our first grandchild." She forcefully nudged Clayton in the side. "Don't we, Clay?"

He hesitated but finally said, "Yeah, sure. We do want the best for our girl. And I'll talk with Robert Mills when he comes over. Promise."

"Katy, we need to examine you now," I told her. "Donna will help you get ready while I step out for a few minutes. Your dad can go to the waiting room until we finish. If you want your mom with you, that's fine. I'll be back when Donna has you all set."

I nodded to Clayton as he followed me into the hallway. "On second thought, there's no one else waiting to be seen. Why don't you come to the break area with me and have a cup of coffee while we wait."

"Sure thing. I need something. I'm trying to hold my emotions in check for Katy's sake, but I feel like I'm gonna explode."

We sat in silence for a few minutes, gazing out the picture window in the break room and watching the neighbor's horses graze in the pasture while we sipped coffee.

Finally Clayton looked at me. "Why are they taking so long? Is something wrong?"

"I'm sure everything is okay. Donna is very good at reassuring expectant mothers, answering questions, and just being an under-standing advocate for these young girls. As a nurse, she also has several things to do: collect a urine, check vital signs, get Katy into a gown, explain a pelvic examination, and on and on."

"I guess so." Clayton took a long sip and sighed. "Tell me something, Doc, what was the youngest girl you've delivered a baby for?"

"Thirteen."

"Thirteen years old? I never heard of such a thing."

"Unfortunately, it's only too true. And believe me, most thirteen-year-old girls are not much beyond the stage of playing with dolls. It's a lost childhood for them."

He shook his head and looked back out the window. "Tell me something else. Isn't it more dangerous for younger girls to have babies?"

"As a matter of fact, it is. Delivery problems are more common. Preeclampsia, which is more commonly known as toxemia of pregnancy, is a greater risk. When these girls are very young and still growing, it can be a major drain on the resources of the body."

"Do you think Katy will be able to have a baby without much trouble? That really worries me."

"That's one of the reasons why I do a pelvic examination. Katy is a normal-sized young lady and probably has an adequate pelvis for normal delivery. Young girls, or even older ones who are very short, worry me the most. Some of them do fine, but others have to have help—for instance, a Caesarean section."

He took another sip, then sat his cup on the table. "Thanks for the coffee and for your time. I guess I'm just a worried old man, but that girl is still my baby daughter. I didn't realize she was growing up so fast." He pushed back from the table and stood up, reaching over to shake hands. "I trust you, Doc. Sometimes you tell me things I don't want to hear,"—he smiled and patted the bulge in his shirt pocket —"like these Camels that I smoke too much, but you've always been honest with me. I know you'll be honest with me when the chips are down. Thanks again for this talk."

Donna entered from the hallway. "We're ready for you now, Doctor."

Clayton nodded at her and headed for the door. "I'll just wait out in the waiting room."

Donna raised her eyebrows at me. "Did you and Clayton have a talk?"

"He just needed to calm down and express his fears. He's really not a bad sort. Just didn't keep tabs on his daughter very well, and he's feeling it now. He considers himself a tough man, but this is a real shock to his ego."

~

IN THE ROOM, I reviewed Katy's vital signs: BP 100/65, pulse 86, respirations 18, temp 98.6, weight 105, height 5 feet 3 inches. Then I did a general exam with attention to her teeth, thyroid, heart, and lungs. The breasts were obviously developing consistent with early pregnancy and the bulge reaching up to just below the navel certainly confirmed the most reasonable diagnosis as intrauterine pregnancy.

In those days, we used an old-fashioned fetoscope to auscultate for fetal heart sounds. I bent over with the scope protruding from my head like a ten-inch unicorn horn and pressed the instrument firmly to the lower abdominal wall while looking at my watch and counting. "Fetal heart rate 144, strong and regular."

The fearful expression on her face resolved into a beautiful smile. "Then the baby's okay? Is a heartbeat of 144 a good sign?"

"A very good sign. Now, Donna will help me with the last part of the exam, to assess your ability to have this baby normally."

Donna assisted as I took routine cultures and a pap smear, then did a manual examination after removing the speculum. Katy's mother sat close by holding her daughter's hand. After I completed the evaluation, Donna helped Katy out of the stirrups and into a sitting position on the cart.

Katy gave a brief smile. "I'm glad that's over. What's the verdict?"

"I would say that you are a very healthy young lady expecting a baby about December the twenty-fifth—a Christmas gift—and that your examination is normal. I expect no problems with a normal labor and delivery."

Katy beamed and even Bonita managed a quick smile. "What's the next step, Doc? You will deliver my baby, won't you?"

"I would be honored to take care of you and your baby, if that's your wish and if your parents agree."

Bonita nodded. "Of course we want you to be her doctor. Just tell us what to do next."

I stood and wrote on a pad of paper, leaning on the pull-down metal shelf. "First, I want Katy to start on these prenatal vitamins. You can get them from the local pharmacist, Barry House, if you like. He makes sure to have an adequate supply of the ones I recommend on hand." I looked at Katy. "Donna will go over dietary recommendations and general health maintenance. We have a booklet on pregnancy I would like you to read. Finally, you need to make an appointment for a recheck in one month. Later in pregnancy, we'll be seeing you on a weekly basis. Also, if anything comes up before your appointment, we're here and expect you to call for any concerns, sudden illnesses, or questions. We want you to have a good outcome, and remember, there are no stupid questions. Understood?"

Katy nodded, and I left them with Donna and made my way back to the break room to relax and finish documenting on the hand-written record. We had a prenatal medical form that I transferred relevant data to so that follow-up visits could be compared quickly and efficiently.

Christine entered the room just as I was finishing. "Everything is caught up. The Harrisons are just getting ready to leave. Okay if I go to lunch now?"

"Of course. When do we start this afternoon?"

"First one up is at 1:15. So you have almost an hour. By the way, Katy said she's going to have a Christmas baby. Is that right?"

"As near as I can tell. She doesn't know her exact dates, but she is about four months along. It's early August, so that should be about right."

Christine clapped her hands. "How exciting. I just love this part of the practice. I'm sorry she got in trouble, but knowing the Harrisons, I believe it will turn out okay. They're a loving and caring family. They'll help her do the right thing. Wow, a Christmas baby."

"Yes, a Christmas baby. Hopefully a healthy one."

CHAPTER 2

$\mathcal{F}$ollowing a long afternoon that day, I picked up the last chart and realized that Robert Mills, Katy's boyfriend, awaited me in my office/conference room. I turned as Donna exited the last exam room. "Is Robert here in regard to Katy's pregnancy?"

"Yes. And he seems very nervous. He wouldn't tell me much, just that he needed to talk with you today. He's actually a late work-in."

"This might take a while, then. When you and Christine finish, you can lock up and leave. If one of you has time, would you please take the night deposit to the bank for me. I need to make a trip back to the hospital after a quick evening meal at home."

"I'll be glad to do that," she said. "Christine is raring to get to a church dinner with some other young people. I'll have her scoot on out as soon as possible."

I took a deep breath and entered the room, greeting Robert with an outstretched hand.

It took a moment for him to look up, notice, and take my hand. The handsome, six-foot-tall, blue-eyed, red-headed seventeen-year-old indeed looked worried. He quickly resumed gazing at the floor while drumming on the arm of the chair with his fingers, his usual cheerful, confident demeanor replaced by an aura of doom.

I sat down on my comfortable brown leather desk chair and

swiveled it about to engage with him. "What can I help you with today?"

He continued to stare at the floor, avoiding eye contact.

"Robert, did you hear my question? I'm here to help."

He finally looked up, but not at me. "Yeah. Well, sorry, Doc. I don't quite know where to begin."

Another uncomfortable silence ensued, until I leaned over and placed my right hand on his left forearm. "I'm your friend, Robert. Anything you say will be kept in strict confidence."

He sighed, finally looking me in the eye, if only briefly. "I guess you know anyway. I really messed up. You saw Katy today. She told me all about it."

"What did she tell you?"

"You know, Doc. About the pregnancy and about us."

Of course I knew, but I wanted him to relax a little and tell me in his own words. "Yes, I know. Why did you come to see me today?"

"Because I need someone to give me advice. I told Dad, and he just blew up. Told me I was stupid, in colorful language I won't repeat. He told me to get out of his sight. I guess he's mad because I mentioned dropping out of school to support a family. Dad was looking forward to me being one of the stars on the football team at Glen Oaks next semester. It would have been my senior year. He said I'm losing my big chance for a football scholarship in college. Said he isn't about to pay for a college education for a worthless failure of a son. I guess I really let him down. I don't know if he'll even let me stay at home. He said something about me packing my things and getting an apartment and a job to support myself."

It sounded to me like perpetually angry Jack Mills, Robert's forty-five-year-old father, had failed his son. "What about your mother? Did you talk to her?"

"I tried. But she heard Dad shouting at me, and all she did was cry. She wouldn't discuss it at all. Told me I would have to make my own decisions. I don't know what she really thinks, but she's afraid to cross Dad. Always has been."

Now I was worried. "Is your father violent with either one of you?"

"Nah, not him. He just likes to yell and vent. I've never seen him lay a hand on Mom, but he puts her down all day long. Makes her feel worthless. But he wouldn't dare touch me. I'm already two inches taller and thirty pounds heavier. I've never threatened him, but he's afraid of anyone he thinks is stronger and bigger."

"I'm sorry your parents are reacting the way they are, but you have disappointed them. You may just be hearing angry words from extremely upset parents."

He looked skeptical. "Maybe, but I'm not counting on it."

"What do you plan to do? You said you wanted advice."

"Katy got me into this situation, now I'm confused."

I frowned. "It takes two to make a baby. It's not fair to put all of the blame on her."

"Sorry. I didn't mean it that way. I take full responsibility for my actions. What I meant was that Katy apparently told you and her folks that I was coming over tonight to ask for her to be my wife. I want to do that, but I'm really scared about how her parents will take it. She admitted that her dad is also angry. I don't know that I'm ready to face them yet."

"What do you intend to do about Katy? Do you really love her?"

"I sure do love her, I think since the seventh grade. She's swell. Beautiful and smart too. I plan to marry her and help raise the baby." He hesitated while I remained silent, waiting for him to continue. "I guess I'm just ashamed to bring disgrace to Katy's family. I want them to like me and approve of me as a worthy son-in-law."

I nodded. "I'm not going to lecture you. You have troubles enough already. What do you want me to give you advice about in this situation?"

"Should I go over to Katy's house and offer marriage tonight? Or should I wait for her dad to settle down?" He gave a little forced smile. "I don't want to get shot by Mr. Harrison, you know."

"He won't shoot you. He may yell, but I hardly think he'll physically harm you."

Robert hung his head. "Nah. He wouldn't do that, but if he does become physical, I won't fight back. I couldn't do anything to hurt

Katy's folks. I'd rather die myself than to bring any kind of hurt into Katy's life. I know now that we should have waited and done things right, but it's too late for that. What do you think I should do tonight?"

"Robert, I don't have all the answers," I said. "This isn't exactly a physical issue, but no less importantly, it's a psychological and spiritual issue. Do you understand?"

He nodded, then made eye contact once again.

"You need to make your decision based on some simple questions about yourself."

"About myself? I don't get it."

"You will. First of all, what kind of man do you want to be? Do you want to be one who takes responsibility for his actions, not just in word but in deed?"

He considered that, then nodded.

"Okay. What kind of memories do you want to have about this issue? Angry families and wife? Disappointment with yourself? Shame at how you faced the problems or ran away from them?"

"I want to believe that I did the right thing by everyone concerned, especially Katy."

"Good. Now you need to face just one thing at a time. You don't even know if the Harrisons will allow Katy to marry you."

Robert's mouth fell open. "You think they might not let us get married?"

"Well, she is just sixteen. I hope you aren't prepared to run off and get married."

"No. No, Doc. We have enough trouble now without making both families hate us."

"Then the thing to do is go to Katy's parents tonight," I advised him. "Apologize for embarrassing and offending them. Pledge your love for Katy, and make it clear that it's not just a physical attraction but real sacrificial love, the kind of love that gives of one's self one hundred percent for the beloved. You do feel that way about Katy, don't you?"

A tear trickled from his eye as he sat slumped over, looking at the floor again. He quickly brushed it away with the back of his hand.

"Yeah. Yeah, sure. That's just the way I feel about Katy. I just didn't know how to express it." He leaned back in his chair with a new look of determination on his face, nodding vigorously.

"Then I expect a full report tomorrow on the outcome. Okay?"

"Okay, but I can't afford to pay you much for your time yet. Maybe when I start working?"

"You just come back at the end of the day tomorrow. There won't be any charge. I suspect you'll be helping Katy pay for her pregnancy care anyway. I don't want to add to your burden."

He stood up and firmly gripped my hand. "I'll do what you said. Then I'll be back tomorrow." He pumped my hand several times, then turned to leave but stopped with his hand on the doorknob and wheeled around.

"Yes?"

"There is one more thing you might do for me. I know you believe in prayer. I'm ashamed to say, but I laughed about you being the 'praying doctor' with some of the fellas one night."

"That's okay. It's a factual statement, but I don't pretend to be a minister."

"I want to ask your forgiveness and ask that you pray for me. I did talk to our minister this afternoon. Reverend White told me to come here, that he couldn't really give me medical advice but he felt you could help me since you're Katy's doctor and familiar with the situation. He also prayed with me, and I found peace. Now I just want Katy to have that same peace and forgiveness. You and Mrs. Matlock, please put us on your prayer list."

"We sure will. You remember to come back tomorrow evening. I'm anxious to know how things are going in your life."

Robert left and hurried down the hallway.

Long shadows were falling with the westering sun the next afternoon. As Donna placed the last patient in the room, I glanced at my watch. Several hours of summer daylight remained, but it was already 6:15. Christine busily cleaned the empty rooms, then came down the hallway carrying a large trash bag filled from the waste baskets. Finally, Donna finished checking vital signs and getting a chief complaint from the remaining patient.

"Did Robert Mills call in today for an appointment?" I asked. "He was supposed to come back for follow-up today."

Christine stopped, thinking back over the very busy day. "I'm pretty sure he didn't call."

"That's disappointing. He promised to get back with me today. Oh well. You never know with these youngsters."

I completed a routine visit with the last patient who needed help with her insulin dosage, then returned to the break room to get a final cup of coffee and complete the documentation on the last patient. I'd just finished writing when the door to the hallway opened and Christine stuck her head in. "Guess who's here?"

"Robert Mills?"

"On the money." She loved wisecracking. "You're sure smart."

"And you're a smart aleck."

She grinned wickedly. "You're so right. Shall I send him in?"

I enjoyed the back and forth with the staff, and they knew it. "If you think it's best."

"What else would you want me to do with him?" She turned with a flourish to go retrieve Robert from the waiting room.

Robert entered and stood waiting to see where we would have our talk.

"Why don't you sit down here at the table," I said. "We're all finished and the ladies will be on their way home in a few minutes."

He nodded and pulled out one of the chairs at our break table, facing the picture window and the view of the horses in the pasture behind the office.

I rose and headed for the coffee pot. "Do you drink coffee?"

"I'm a coffee addict."

"Want a cup?"

"Sure. Make it black and strong."

I chuckled. "It's been sitting about three hours. I think I can guarantee the 'strong' part."

"Suits me fine. Sorry to be late, but I just got off work."

"Really?"

"Really. I took your advice. I want to be a responsible man. So I went right to the feed mill and applied for a job. I'm loading fifty-pound feed bags on the farmers' trucks when they pull in to pick up an order. It's hard work but pays fairly well for a young guy."

"That's great. You landed that job pretty quick."

"Yeah. It didn't hurt that Mr. Terry, the manager, is friends with my dad. I think Dad even put in a good word for me. I never expected that to happen."

I smiled. Jack Mills wouldn't want his reputation in the community spoiled by a wayward son. I didn't doubt that he had used his influence, but I didn't voice my suspicion to Robert. "You seem much more relaxed. Tell me what happened during the visit last night."

He smiled, sat his cup down, and leaned forward with his forearms resting on the table, hands loosely clasped beside his cup. "I think it turned out good, but I want your opinion. Here's what happened…"

"Good evening, Mrs. Harrison. May I come in and have a word with you and your husband?"

Mrs. Harrison opened the door, a blank expression on her face, then nodded and motioned me into the living room, where Katy's dad sat reading the evening newspaper. Katy peeked around the hallway entrance to the living room while Mr. Harrison folded his newspaper and tossed it onto the coffee table.

Mr. Harrison glanced at Katy. "Go to your room. You aren't needed in here. If we want you, we'll call you." He turned steely eyes on me and pointed at a chair across the room.

Mrs. Harrison took a seat on the blue sofa across from me as I sat down.

For at least a minute, maybe more, no one said anything. Then Mr. Harrison cleared his throat, leaned forward with his hands on his knees, and stared at me. "Well?"

I assumed that was my cue to talk, but my first words came out in a garbled jumble of squeaking sounds.

He held up his hand. "Whoa, boy. You're gonna have to do better than that. I can't understand a word you said."

I took a deep breath, then slowly said, "Yes, sir. Sorry, sir."

Mr. Harrison sat back and relaxed a little while I found my voice.

My mind went blank for a few seconds, but suddenly I found the courage to speak. "First, I want to apologize to you and your wife, and to Katy, for causing this situation."

Mr. Harrison nodded but said nothing.

"Second, I want all three of you to know that I really do love Katy. I know my action was inexcusable, but I'm hoping you can find it in your hearts to forgive me." The room remained silent, so I went on with my speech, but it didn't come out like I rehearsed it at all. Maybe it was just as well. "Finally, I would like to marry Katy and be a father to the baby."

Still no response. Just grim stares.

I completely forgot my speech. Instead I blurted out, "Whether you consent to our marriage or not, I will work and pay for her prenatal care and for the baby when it comes and as it grows up. Maybe someday I'll be able to prove myself worthy of your daughter."

Mr. Harrison apparently saw my sincerity, because he relaxed a little more. "Robert—or do you want to be called Bob?"

"Whichever you please, sir."

"All right, Robert, how are you going to accomplish all of this with no job and no education? You see, it's my daughter and her baby we're talking about. I have a right to know the answers."

"Yes, sir. I agree fully. Yesterday, I went to the county seat at Glen Falls and applied at the adult school center for an application so I can complete my GED degree for a high-school-equivalent diploma. Next, I went to see Reverend White and prayed to find forgiveness for the wrong I committed against you and your family. Last of all, I went to see Dr. Matlock, and he advised me to come and have a man-to-man talk with you. He asked me what kind of man I wanted to be, and that got me thinking very seriously about my life. I guess I haven't done much of that in the past. I admit to being a selfish person, but I will do better in the future."

I stopped talking for a minute, and no one said anything, so I went on, "I guess you can believe me or not, but by the grace of God, I'm going to do what's right from here on out."

Mr. Harrison glanced at his wife, and she nodded at him. "Okay, son. I won't say that I'm not angry with both you and Katy for what you did. But never let it be said that I wouldn't give a man a second chance." He looked at Mrs. Harrison again. "Go call Katy. Have her join us."

And just like that, Katy was standing at my side, expressing her love and total commitment to me for life.

Mr. Harrison shook my hand and said, "If you're going to be part of the family, come on in and join us for dinner. We were about ready to eat when you knocked on the door."

Mrs. Harrison smiled a little and gave me a hug, but best of all, Katy took my hand and led me to their dining room, where her little brother, Ken, sat making faces at us when his parents weren't looking.

"That's quite a story, Robert," I said. "I'm impressed with how you're living up to your word already. Anytime you or Katy need to talk, feel free to come in with her during her appointments, or maybe meet me at the soda fountain at Barry House's pharmacy."

"We sure will, Doc. Thanks for everything."

"One more thing before you go. When's the wedding?"

"In two weeks. It's going to be a private affair with just our families and Reverend White having us say our vows. I put a down payment on an apartment here in town today. We'll live there until I can do better. Dad actually let me borrow a little money to do that. And Katy and I would be honored if you and Mrs. Matlock could attend the wedding."

"We'll sure try to keep the date open. Thanks for the invitation."

"You were sure right. It's best to face problems head on, man to man, so to speak. I owe you a lot for your advice."

I watched as Robert climbed into his jalopy—a faded-red 1960 Chevy sedan that had seen better days—fired up the engine, and drove off with a smile on his face as he waved out his window.

It was true that they had blundered, changing what could have been a proper wedding celebration and promising start to life together, but there was still a lot of potential wrapped up in those two young lives so filled with hopes and dreams for the future. I was so happy that they had found the God of second chances.

CHAPTER 3

The last week of August 1974 found me in Glen Falls, on call for hospital admissions and making early morning rounds. I had seven patients to see: four on the medical floor, one on the post-op surgical floor, and a new mother and baby on the OB ward. I'd just started reading the first chart on the medical floor when the operator switched on the overhead paging system with a familiar popping sound that always proceeded an announcement. "Dr. Matlock, call the emergency room. Dr. Matlock, call the emergency room."

Sighing, I picked up the phone in the doctors' dictation room on the medical floor and dialed ER. The familiar voice of Ann Kilgore, nursing supervisor, came on the line. "Good morning, Ann. This is Dr. Matlock."

"Good morning. Can you hold for a moment? Dr. Hayden has a patient he needs to discuss with you."

"Sure thing." I continued to review the first chart while holding the silent receiver next to my ear. The days of music while on hold hadn't yet arrived at our county hospital.

A click alerted me that Dr. Hayden had finally picked up the phone to deliver his message, so I laid my chart on the desk.

"Jerry Hayden here. Dr. Matlock?"

"Yes, I'm all ears, Jerry. What's up?"

"I've got this young guy, Michael Richardson, twenty-three years old, with a rip-roaring lobar pneumonia. He's from here in town but doesn't have a doctor. I've already got blood cultures and lab work going for you. It's really busy this morning, so I need you to come down and take care of him. Four victims from an MVA just rolled through the doors."

"Sure, Jerry. I'll be right there. Are his vital signs stable?"

"They are right now, but he doesn't look good. That's another reason I called for your help."

"I'm on my way. See you in a minute."

Arriving in the ER, I passed through the congested main receiving area, entered room 2, and saw Ann Kilgore taping an IV in place while motioning for me to look at the vital signs on the bedside monitor: BP 90/58, pulse 120. I stepped to the cart where the gravely ill young man sat with his head and upper body elevated at sixty degrees, obviously anxious, struggling to breathe. Although diaphoretic and mildly cyanotic, he attempted a smile and reached for my hand.

Taking his clammy hand, I returned the smile. "You must be Michael Richardson."

He nodded.

"I'm Dr. Matlock. I'm told you have pneumonia. How long have you been sick?"

Answering only in brief phrases, he attempted to tell me his story. "Sick three days. Lots worse today. Mowed small yard for my neighbor three days ago, but unable to do anything since. Coughed my head off until I had a splitting headache." He stopped talking, continuing to fight for each breath, coughing and hacking, obviously fearful and exhausted.

"Michael, you just lie still. We'll talk later when you feel more up to it. Right now, I'm going to do a quick examination so we can get you started on treatment."

At that moment, a young woman holding a baby and followed by two young children entered the room. She was thin, almost emaciated, with a dazed, apathetic appearance. Her blond hair, naturally long eyelashes, blue eyes, and fair complexion revealed that she had been a great beauty in the not-too-distant past.

"This is Mrs. Richardson," Ann Kilgore said. "Maybe she can tell you more about what's going on with her husband."

I quickly introduced myself and directed her and the children to nearby chairs that Ann brought in for them. "I was just telling your husband that I'm going to do a quick examination so he can be started on treatment. After I take a quick listen to his heart and lungs, why don't you tell me what's been going on."

She nodded.

Michael had extensive rales and expiratory wheezes along with diminished breath sounds throughout the entire right lower chest and corresponding area of the back, consistent with the stated diagnosis of lobar pneumonia, obviously affecting the lower lobe of his right lung. His breathing continued to be very labored, and sweat plastered down his dark hair. Light-blue eyes gazed at me imploringly, pleading for relief. The remainder of the exam revealed no abnormalities of the abdomen or extremities, other than mild cyanosis of the feet and hands. He was on oxygen per nasal canula at 4 liters a minute, but appeared to be nearing impending shock.

I began barking orders as Ann Kilgore jotted quick notes on a clip-board tablet. "Give 1 liter of normal saline as a bolus stat, then recheck vital signs and call results. Start Cephalexin at 2 grams IV piggyback, then 1 gram IV piggyback every four hours. Change oxygen from nasal canula to oxygen mask with the flow set at 6 liters per minute. Obtain arterial blood gases twenty minutes after changing to oxygen mask administration. Finally, ICU room if at all possible."

Glancing at the chart Ann handed me as she hurried from the room to initiate the orders, I noted his temperature of 104 and respirations of 32. I squeezed Michael's shoulder, smiled as reassuringly as I could, and took a seat near his wife. "Mrs. Richardson, I'll examine your husband more thoroughly once we get him in the ICU. I need to know more about him and his illness. He's too sick to give me much information right now."

"I know."

"How long has he been sick?"

She looked puzzled for a moment. "Maybe three or four days. I don't know for sure."

My mystified expression must have been noticed by Michael. He shook his head and looked with sadness at his family.

She looked at him, then back to me. "I wasn't home for a couple of days. Just got back yesterday and found him like that."

"So you and the children were away visiting and you don't know for sure?"

She looked at her oldest. "Do you know how long Daddy's been sick, Wendy?"

"She was home with him?" I asked.

"All of 'em were home with him. Anything wrong with that?"

"I didn't say so. Just trying to get information about his illness. What did you say your name is, Mrs. Richardson?"

"I didn't say."

"Oh, sorry. I didn't mean to offend you."

"It's okay. My name's Marilyn, and I don't care what you know about us. I had Wendy when I was fifteen and Michael was sixteen. We had to get married. Now there's two more. Howie's four and Jimmy's one. I have to get away and rest sometimes. Michael takes care of the kids when I'm gone."

Not sure where the conversation was headed, I turned to their daughter. "Wendy, is that your name?"

She looked up but quickly lowered her eyes again. Very softly she said, "I'm Wendy."

"That's a pretty name. It fits a very pretty little girl."

Wendy smiled and looked up at me. "Thanks, mister. You're pretty too."

I tried to maintain a serious look. "Can you tell me how long your Daddy's been sick?"

"Several days, I think. Don't know for sure."

"Was he able to care for you up until today? He seems very sick today."

"He fixed our food till today. Mama gave us cereal this morning."

Marilyn looked uncomfortable with the questioning, so I stood up and excused myself. "I'm going to look at Michael's X-rays with the radiologist. Your husband will be going to a room soon. I'll be back to check him again and let you know how he's doing."

She gave a barely perceptible nod, and I left the room.

Ann Kilgore met me by the nurses' station. "I wanted to warn you about her. She is a frequent flyer here, always wanting narcotics. I don't know what she's had today, but I'm sure she's on something."

"That's really sad. And Michael? Is he also abusing drugs?"

"I don't believe so. He brings the children in whenever they're sick. She never accompanies him. He seems to be keeping everything going on his own."

"Are they going to be safe with her while he's hospitalized?"

"Doc, I'm pretty sure she wouldn't purposely harm them, but neglect them? Well, that's another story. Some of the staff have known her for years. I might persuade one of our aides to look after them while Michael's sick. I'm sure Marilyn wouldn't mind. She'll be off on another drug-and-alcohol bender as soon as she can get away. It's such a shame. She started out being a good mother, but I believe the stress of financial problems along with family responsibility is too much for her now."

Shaking my head in dismay, I went to review the chest X-ray.

ENCOUNTERING one of the X-ray techs, I learned that our hospital radiologist, Dr. Strong, had finished with the special procedures for the day and could be found in the radiology reading room, where he sat reviewing the films of the day. As I entered the semi-dark room illuminated only by backlighting from several radiology view boxes, I greeted him.

He turned his swivel chair toward me and smiled. "I bet I know which film you're looking for, Carl."

"Michael Richardson's portable chest X-ray."

He turned back around to sort through a pile of folders. "Just as I thought. I reviewed it a couple of minutes ago." After quickly retrieving the portable AP (anterior-posterior) view of the chest, he mounted it back on the view box. "Quite impressive, wouldn't you say?"

"I'll say. It looks like the entire right lower lobe of the lung is involved in lobar consolidation."

"That's exactly right. The right lower lobe isn't collapsed. It's just completely socked in with a lobar pneumonic process. My guess is that it's pneumococcal pneumonia. This guy is pretty young according to the ID on the film. Is he immunosuppressed?"

"Not that I'm aware of, but I just met him. I'm on call and he's already my first admission of the day."

"Well, good luck to both him and you. Judging by this film, he appears to be seriously ill."

"You're right about that. I'm putting him in ICU. Thanks for your time."

"My pleasure. I hope your patient does well."

I hurried back to the ER to check on my patient.

Ann Kilgore appeared as harried as ever with a crush of morning patients, the volume increased by MVA (motor vehicle accident) victims. As I approached, she looked up from the desk where she had just placed a stack of orders from one of our surgeons. "Jan Hart just took your patient up to the second-floor ICU via the elevator. She's the aide I mentioned who might help with the children. She's their next-door neighbor and has known Michael since he was a little boy. Her husband passed away years ago, and I think the Richardson family is her own special project."

"That's good of her if she can help." I turned to leave.

"Wait. I almost forgot. Lab just brought over his results." She handed me a stack of lab slips, which I quickly perused.

Hemoglobin 15.0, hematocrit 45, WBC (white blood count) 29,500 with 95% polymorphonuclear leukocytes. BUN (blood urea nitrogen) 35, creatinine 1.5, electrolytes within normal limits. No other abnormalities. Sputum gram stain loaded with Gram-positive diplococci and WBCs. Culture pending. Blood cultures x 2 pending.

"That about clinches it, Ann. He has a rip-roaring pneumococcal pneumonia with dehydration, and I have little doubt that he's septic with impending shock. He's going to require an extraordinary level of care to recover from this insult to his body."

"I'm afraid you're right. Anyway, here comes Jan now."

Jan Hart arrived pushing the now-empty ER cart.

"Jan, you know Dr. Matlock, don't you?"

"I sure do. How are you doin', Doc? You have one sick little cookie there. I've known Michael since he was knee-high to a grasshopper. Always knocking on my back door wanting to do chores so I'd give him a cookie. I got in the habit of calling him Cookie, but he didn't seem to mind. I just wish he hadn't got mixed up with that no-account wife of his. He was always a good boy, very respectful and polite. Well, that's just so much water under the bridge, as they say."

"I need to hurry up and see him, but what will happen with his children if his wife isn't responsible?"

Jan put her hands on her hips and straightened to her full height. "Never you mind worryin' about that. Those are good kids. Michael's been trying so hard to teach them right. Got his work cut out, cause she's been showing them how to live wrong. I'll keep them at my house if she takes off again. I'm already halfway expectin' her to come ask me to do just that after I get off work this afternoon."

"Thanks, Mrs. Hart. That's good of you."

"Jan's the name, Doctor. Just plain Jan."

"Okay, Jan it is." With that, I headed to the ICU to see Michael.

THEY HAD a good crew working today, head nurse Linda Ottinger, ICU nurses Peggy Wilson and Liz O'Conner, and two nurses' aides. I sat down at the desk after glancing at the monitor across the room, relieved that the IV saline appeared to be having the desired effect. The nurses were working with Michael, setting up his bedside monitors and seeing to his comfort. His BP was up to 125/84 with the pulse down to 93 and respirations 24. He appeared a little more alert with less cyanosis now that he had been on more oxygen for a few minutes.

I picked up the phone and called my office.

On the second ring, Christine's pleasant voice came over the line. "Dr. Matlock's office. How can I help you?"

"It's me, Christine. I'm tied up at the hospital once again. I have a critical patient with lobar pneumonia and sepsis."

"Oh, really? Anyone I know?"

"I don't think so. This is a new patient admitted from ER. I'm on call today."

"I forgot. I bet you won't be able to get here for a while. Is that it?"

I chuckled. "You've got the routine down pat, don't you?"

"I know your habits pretty well by now. What do you want me to do about the schedule?"

"I'll try to be there by about one o'clock. See how many you can move to later this week, or to this afternoon if they insist. Is Donna there yet?"

"Funny you should ask. She just walked in."

"Great. She can help you with the schedule. Then the two of you take a nice leisurely lunch hour if possible."

"Right. Consider it done. Keep us informed if you need to make more changes. Looks like mainly routine visits this afternoon. Shouldn't be hard to reschedule. See you later."

I placed the handset back on the phone and glanced through Michael's old hospital chart, mostly routine ER visits in the past. No previous admissions. As soon as the nurses finished making him comfortable and attaching all the monitor devices and leads, I crossed the room to examine him more thoroughly. "How are you feeling now? Any better?"

Michael smiled and nodded.

"I've been studying your hospital record. Looks like you've been in fairly good health in the past. I know you're still short of breath. You can shake your head yes or no to most of the questions I'm going to ask now. We'll no doubt talk a lot more as you get better. Okay?"

He nodded.

"According to your chart, you've been to the ER several times in the last four years, mainly for minor problems. Sore throats, flu, an ankle sprain, a toe fracture. I assume that you're usually healthy?"

Michael nodded again.

"I didn't find any list of medications or allergies, just like your ER chart today documented."

Another nod.

"Now, count with your fingers if you still feel too short of breath to talk much. How many days have you been sick?"

He shrugged at first, then hesitantly held up three, then four fingers.

"Four days?"

Michael nodded.

"You have a serious case of pneumonia now. That's why you're in the ICU. Have you ever had pneumonia in the past?"

He shook his head.

"Any other serious illnesses, ever?"

Once again, he shook his head.

"Were you too sick to work last week?"

At that, he looked down at the sheets and sighed. Finally looking back up, he mouthed the words, "Out of work."

"I'm sorry. You mean you're laid off work at present?"

His face flushed as he nodded and looked down again. "Do odd jobs now, like mowing grass."

I felt uncomfortable for having asked him. "Look, it's nothing to be ashamed of. The economy's not too good now. A lot of people are laid off from work."

With a sad expression, he made eye contact and nodded.

"I'm going to examine you more thoroughly now that you're breathing a little better. I'll want to look in your ears and throat, listen to your heart and lungs, check your abdomen, your extremities, and your reflexes. It won't take too long, but it'll give me a lot of information about how you're doing. Ready?"

He managed a wan smile, nodded, and spoke softly. "Okay, Doctor. Go ahead."

About twenty minutes later, I finished a complete examination except for detailed neurological testing, then sat down by his bedside to discuss the findings. "Michael, you're on the thin side, but other than that and pneumonia, you seem healthy. I won't mislead you about your condition. You're seriously ill, but you appear to have a basically healthy constitution. I fully expect you to recover. You're already showing signs of improvement. Your vital signs are stabilizing with improving blood pressure, pulse, and respirations. But I would be greatly surprised if you aren't in ICU for the better part of a week. You're going to need to be patient with your recovery."

He looked very distressed, so I went on, "I'm sorry if I upset you. I'm being very truthful when I say that I expect you to get well. It's just going to be slow."

Michael shook his head and with effort said, "It's not what you said. I just don't have any insurance or any money for this. That's all."

"Look. I don't want you worrying. Emotional stress is hard on the body, particularly when a person is fighting a serious infection or any other major illness. I'll contact our social worker, Jane Dobson. She specializes in helping people. Our hospital is a not-for-profit organization. Each year, it's required to commit to a certain amount of charitable assistance for the citizens of our community. I'm pretty sure she can work this out for you."

He shook his head. "Don't want charity. Just time to pay bills."

"Whatever you say. But please, just let her take a shot at this for you. Think of it as for your family. You need to put food on the table, the hospital has community obligations, and you're out of work and deserve the assistance. Just give it a try, okay?"

He looked undecided at first, but finally gave a fleeting smile, reached up, and shook my hand. "Thanks, Doctor."

"You're welcome, Mr. Richardson. Now let's get you well and back on your feet."

I FINALLY FINISHED rounds and looked in on Michael Richardson one last time. Satisfied with his progress, I headed for the office. I had just enough time for a quick hamburger and a Diet Coke while driving, then needed five minutes before starting work to talk to Christine and Donna. They truly cared for our patients and wouldn't be able to rest or function until they knew all the details.

CHAPTER 4

$\mathcal{A}$fter finishing early morning hospital rounds, I had a little extra time and drove along country backroads to the office in order to mentally prepare for the day. Farm fields bearing rows of gently waving golden-brown cornstalks, peacefully grazing horses and cattle, and late-season cuttings of fragrant hay always relaxed me. September 3, the day after Labor Day, promised to be a full day. Tuesdays mornings were reserved for OB patients, along with postpartum visits for new mothers and their babies. Tuesday afternoons were for routine and emergency patients. No doubt there would be many waiting to be seen due to the holiday weekend.

As I drove, I couldn't help but ruminate on the visit with Michael Richardson. He had recovered enough to be discharged after seven days of hospitalization, three in ICU and four on the medical floor. Our social worker had indeed come through for him. The hospital had written off his medical bill as charity.

I replayed the visit in my mind as I drove.

"You look like a new man today, Michael," I said. "How are you feeling?"

"Much better, thanks to you. I can breathe okay now. It's a good thing I quit smoking a few months ago. Couldn't afford to buy cigarettes anyway."

"Your lungs sound completely normal this morning, and the last chest X-ray done yesterday afternoon showed no further signs of pneumonia."

He nodded. "That's great, Doc. I do have a question. Would you be willing to take care of my family? The social worker, Jane Dobson, helped me get in contact with the Medicaid office for my kids. They're pretty healthy, but they're all behind on immunizations and check-ups."

"I'd be happy to see you and your family. I was just going to tell you that I need to see you in about a week to recheck your lungs. You're to take oral Keflex for another three days and get plenty of rest."

He smiled ruefully. "I'm pretty likely to get rest for a little while. I just do odd jobs. It'll take a few days to line up more work."

"Will you be able to get to my office in Glen Oaks?"

"I know where it is, but I'll have to get a buddy to bring me. I'm pretty sure I can get a ride."

"Don't you have transportation?"

"When I was laid off a few months ago, I had to let my car go back to the dealer. I usually walk most places."

"Do you have family locally besides your wife and children?"

"No. My folks are dead. We don't have any close relatives in the area anymore."

How unfortunate. "Is someone going to pick you up from the hospital this morning?"

He sighed. "No. I'll be fine. I only live a mile away. I'll walk home."

"Would you like the social worker to try to line up transportation for you? She has a list of volunteer drivers since we don't have bus or taxi service in town."

"No, but thanks for asking. I really couldn't accept any more charity. Everyone here has been swell to me and my family."

I didn't say anything about it, but I knew from Ann Kilgore that his wife was gone again and no one knew where she was. Jan Hart had taken over babysitting the Richardson children. He had to know that, but I didn't want to embarrass him.

As I stuck out my hand, he took it and gave a warm handshake. "Thanks again, Doctor. I believe you saved my life, and I owe you for that."

"I'm just glad you're getting well and can return to your home and family."

I HAD BEEN TROUBLED as I exited the hospital that morning. There were so many needs in the community that had little to do with medicine or medical care, but my resources seemed so limited in regard to the panorama of human suffering. As I pulled into my parking space at the back of the office, I breathed a quick prayer for the Michael Richardson family.

I encountered Donna in the lab/break room. "Good morning. Are you ready for a big day following the three-day weekend?"

She laughed. "I'm ready, and you'd better be. There are already six OB patients here and twelve more due this morning, counting one postpartum visit. Enjoy your coffee while I start putting them in rooms."

I relaxed, taking her advice and enjoying my first cup of Folgers dark brew for the morning. Within a few minutes she handed me the first chart, and I began seeing patients posthaste.

By the time two hours had rolled by, I had seen thirteen repeat visits with five to go until the noon hour. I hastened to the lab while Donna prepped the next patient for examination. I already felt the need for a caffeine boost since my day had started at 5:30.

Christine entered while I sipped my coffee. "Mind if I join you? Everyone is here and checked in for the morning session."

I nodded, knowing quite well that curiosity also had a bearing on her entrance to the break area.

Christine poured her cup, all the while keeping her head cocked toward the wall-mounted extension phone, but it remained silent for once. She hovered nearby as I finished my refreshing cup. "Mrs. Mills is your next patient."

I glanced up. "Mrs. Mills? Oh, you mean Katy."

"You got it, Doc. Katy's mom came with her. It looks like the family situation is settling down. You and Mrs. Matlock attended the wedding ceremony, didn't you?"

"Yes. Now let me guess, you want to know all about it, am I right?"

She pulled out the chair across from me and placed her mug on the table. "You know I do. Now, please, don't keep me waiting."

I grinned. "You win, but there really isn't much to tell. The ceremony took place at the parsonage in Reverend White's living room. The Harrisons and the Millses were the only ones there besides my wife and me. Robert wore his best dark-gray suit and Katy wore a pretty blue dress with matching shoes and purse. She had a beautiful bouquet of red and white roses that both families pitched in to buy. After it was all over, the young couple left for their honeymoon, which again the families provided by paying for two nights in a hotel in downtown Indianapolis. Probably not your idea of a great romantic getaway, huh?"

"It sounds fine to me," she responded with great solemnity. "Maybe a trip to Europe would have been more to my taste, but still, very nice indeed. But you left out some important details."

I raised my eyebrows, wondering what was coming next. Knowing Christine, it could be anything.

"What about the rice, cans tied to the back of the car? In fact, what car did they take to Indy? Surely not Robert's old junker?"

I held up both hands. "Okay. Okay. So I left out a few details."

She put her coffee cup down, sighed, and leaned forward, elbows on the table, fingers intertwined, and chin resting on her hands. "Please, Doc, go on already. Weddings are just so, so romantic."

I pushed my chair back and stood to return to work. "We threw rice at them as they ran to their car parked in Reverend White's driveway. They drove off in the Harrisons' best car, the blue 1972 Buick, and there were cans tied to the bumper. They made quite a racket as

35

Robert drove off with both of them smiling and waving back at us." I took a deep breath. "And before you ask, they're living in that upstairs apartment on Main Street in the building beside the post office. Is there anything else you want to know?"

The phone rang, interrupting our conversation.

Christine jumped up to grab it off the wall, and I escaped to the hallway. I had to chuckle, knowing that would frustrate her a good deal. Christine could be a little overbearing in her quest to know everything about our patients, but I knew she dearly loved people. In fact, she and Donna were two of the drawing cards, bringing new patients in to experience their genuine interest and hospitality. They indeed made our patients feel at home.

DONNA ALREADY HAD the first two exam rooms ready and was putting another patient in room 3 near the end of the hallway when I picked up the next chart, labeled Katherine Mills. I smiled and entered to greet Katy and her mom. "How are you folks doing today?" I stuck out my hand to Katy first.

She briefly clasped my hand in both of hers. "Robert and I want to thank you and Mrs. Matlock for attending our wedding. It meant so much to us. We had a lovely time in Indianapolis, paid for by our families, no less. Be sure and give my love to your wife, and thanks to both of you for the lovely wall plaque, 'Bless This Home.'"

I took a seat beside the examination table. "Are you doing okay physically?"

"Yes, I'm over all the morning sickness, eating well, taking my vitamins, walking in the evenings with Robert, and generally feeling well."

"I'm glad to hear that. Are you feeling much movement by the baby."

"I'll say she is," Bonita Harrison said. "Keeps grabbing my hand when she's at our house, wanting me to feel the baby move too. It does seem to be a very active little thing."

Katy beamed. "I'm so glad to feel the life inside me. The love I already have for the baby makes me realize just how much my mother loves me too. There's nothing like it."

After exchanging pleasantries for a little while, I proceeded with the examination. "Your BP is 98/65 with a pulse of 90. Your weight is up three pounds from a month ago. There is no sign of protein in the urine or swelling in your lower extremities. That's all very good." I pulled out the extension at the foot of the table. "If you can just lie back with your head on the pillow, I'll pull the sheet down far enough to examine your abdomen and listen to the baby's heartbeat."

I measured the fundal height in regard to the umbilicus, only a rough estimate of gestational age but nevertheless valuable as a marker of advancing pregnancy. "The uterine fundus is just at the level of the umbilicus, about twenty-four weeks along. I believe you told me your periods were irregular, but the fundal height is still consistent with a late-December birth."

"That's right. Sometimes my periods are irregular. I didn't worry until I was well over a month late."

I listened to the fetal heartbeat, observing the second hand of my watch and counting. "Heart beat 128, strong and regular." I removed the fetoscope from my head. "You and the baby seem to be progressing very well. Any questions?"

Katy shook her head. "The book your nurse gave me to read answered most of my questions. I don't have any just now."

I picked up her chart, preparing to leave the room. "Assuming no problems before then, I'll see you in one month."

Bonita smiled reassuringly at Katy, then followed me into the hallway while Katy got dressed. "Thanks for taking good care of our daughter and for helping our family transition through a difficult time. Clayton is doing his best to be a good friend to Robert. Katy didn't tell you, but she and Robert are starting the adult education classes this evening in Glen Falls to get their GEDs. Clayton is letting them use his car to get there and back. That clunker Robert drives isn't very reliable."

"Bonita, I'm sorry for the way things happened, and I know that you are also. But you folks are handling it very well, all things considered."

"Thanks again, Doctor. We'll see you next month. I hope you don't mind. Katy wants me to come with her for the visits."

"Not at all. You're very welcome to come. If she has any problems, don't hesitate to contact me."

CHAPTER 5

"I'm worried about your new patient, Michael Richardson." Christine stood shaking her head sadly.

I had just entered the lab with fifteen minutes to spare before the day began in earnest at 9:00. "Why? Is he worse?"

"I don't think so, but he just called to tell me that he didn't know if he could make his appointment this afternoon. He asked me to move him to the end of the day so that it wouldn't inconvenience anyone else if he couldn't get here."

"Did he say why?"

"That's what makes it so sad. His buddy can't get off work to get him here in time. Michael sounded very disappointed. He apologized several times. He was so soft spoken, just didn't want to inconvenience our regular patients. He also canceled the appointment for his three children. They were supposed to start catching up on their immunizations today."

"I'm sorry to hear that, but maybe he'll be able make the later appointment. I really need to see him in follow-up."

"Don't be mad now, Doc. I told him to come in at six if he could. And to bring his kids. I promised that you'd see them anyway. Okay?"

I tried to suppress a grin. "That's an hour after quitting time. Quite the softy, aren't you?"

"You know we never finish much before six. I hoped you wouldn't mind. If you say so, I'll call him back and reschedule them for another day."

I assumed a severe look. "You didn't consult me or Donna. You just assumed we'd be happy to live with your decision, that neither one of us had other plans for this evening."

Christine bowed her head, clasped her hands together, at a loss for words for once.

She looked so distressed that I hurried on, "Just kidding, Christine. I appreciate that you're willing to inconvenience yourself for others. But, seriously, you need to be sure Donna will stay over to give the vaccines. And for my part, yes, it's okay if she's willing to help us. You know I'm a softy too."

Christine's transformation was a wonder to behold. She did a 360-degree whirl, stood up on her tiptoes, clapped her hands, and shouted. "Yippee. I knew you'd agree. Actually, Donna and I have been dying to meet this new family. She already said it was okay with her."

I should have known that, but before I could say a word, she whirled back around and dashed out the door to the reception area, bearing the good news to Donna.

Donna began cleaning rooms at 5:45 while I finished my charting and Christine balanced the books. Still no sign of the Richardsons, but then Michael had been told to come at 6:00. My paperwork completed, I stood while glancing at the clock on the wall. It was 6:07 and no one else had arrived. I took the charts to Christine for filing and noted the consternation on her face. "No more calls from our last patient?"

"None at all, Doc. But thanks for being a good sport."

Donna returned from tidying the exam rooms. "Look outside, you two. There's a car just pulling into the lot."

Gravel crunched as a tan early 1960s Ford sedan parked, emitting a cloud of black smoke from the exhaust pipe as the driver killed the engine. The bent front side panel and fender proved that the vehicle had seen better days. Michael exited the passenger door, opened the back door to retrieve a small child, and two other children spilled out the other side of the car as the driver held the other door open for them.

Michael's friend remained outside, pulled a pack of cigarettes from his shirt pocket, smiled, and waved at the ladies as they opened the door to help Michael with the children.

I turned to go back to the break room, calling over my shoulder, "Let me know when you have them ready. I'm going to finish the coffee in the carafe. It's still hot and probably extra-strong by now."

FIFTEEN MINUTES LATER, Donna opened the door to the break room. "I put them all in your conference room. It's the only one big enough to comfortably keep them together. Christine's back there holding little Jimmy. He's thirteen months but small and frail appearing for his age. Jimmy doesn't say many words, and his dad says he's not walking yet either."

"Christine loves children. I know she misses her younger siblings in Michigan."

"I believe that's why she wanted them to come in so much. But, whew! That little Howie is a handful. He's only four, but his dad has to keep pulling him away from your desk. He dearly wants to explore the drawers. And seven-year-old Wendy with those blue eyes and that wavy blond hair is already a little beauty. I'll bet her mother is very pretty."

"I saw her briefly at the hospital a couple of times, but that's a sad story. She is addicted to narcotics and probably other drugs. The ER knows her very well. Did Michael mention anything about her?"

"Only that she's out of town today. He really didn't seem open to talking about her, so I let it drop."

I sighed. "Okay. Let's go see them. We'll take care of the children first. After their immunizations are given, you and Christine can take them to the waiting room while I talk with Michael."

Donna smiled. "Sounds like a plan. I'm sure we'll enjoy that part of the visit. Let's do it, Doctor."

41

THE CHILDREN WERE INDEED BEHIND on immunizations. Little Jimmy hadn't had any vaccines, and the others were way behind. After their examinations, Donna gave them their shots, and the older two only whimpered a little. Little Jimmy squalled but soon quieted as Christine rocked him in her arms and held him close. The ladies took the little ones to the waiting room while I remained to talk with Michael.

"Michael, we need to keep an eye on Jimmy. I'd like to see him back in a month. He's a little behind on growth and seems to have some developmental delays. He may need referral to a specialist if he continues to have problems. It's best to take care of potential problems as early as possible."

"Thanks, Doctor. I'll do my best to get him here. I know he doesn't seem quite right, but it's a long story."

"Do you want to tell me about it?"

Michael leaned forward, folded his hands in his lap, and looked away from me. I remained silent, waiting on a signal to either proceed with the conversation or drop it for now.

Finally, he let out a long breath and looked back at me. "I guess so. You probably know or suspect the problem in our family anyway. It's my wife. She rarely interacts with Jimmy, lets him lay in wet diapers and cry. He doesn't get much attention from her. For that matter, neither do the other two anymore. Oh, she isn't mean to any of them. Just ignores them when she's home, which is less and less these days."

"Do you think that's the problem with Jimmy's development?"

"I don't know for sure, but I have to suspect it's at least part of the trouble. Just not enough interaction between them."

I nodded and waited for him to continue.

"I don't want you to think Marilyn's all bad, Doc. She used to be a good mother. In some ways I blame myself, and I know she blames me."

I raised my eyebrows. "How so?"

"Ever since I lost my job, I'm seldom home until the kids are already in bed. I do odd jobs, cut grass, do simple repairs, anything to keep food on the table. It's not like I got fired. I was laid off along with about fifteen other workers. Our company made special engine parts for Chrysler. When the economy started to go south, we were called in and told of necessary sacrifices." He couldn't keep the bitterness from his voice. "Workers from every department were laid off. I was the low man on the totem pole in maintenance, so here I am. No job and not much money. I have little else to lose but my pride."

Sharing in his sorrow, I was at a loss for words. Finally, I asked, "How do you care for the children when she's not home?"

"She leaves them with the neighbor, Jan Hart. If it wasn't for her, I don't know what I'd do. She's a grandmotherly type, a good soul and a lifesaver for my kids."

"Is there something we can do to help your wife? Would she come in for an appointment with you and the children?"

He shook his head. "I doubt it, Doc. She got together with some old girlfriends, had a few drinks, and everything went downhill from there. Now that's all she wants to do: party, drink with friends, and take Morphine or whatever she can get on the street."

I didn't know what to say. After an uncomfortable pause, I asked about his transportation. "Will your friend be able to bring you and the children for future appointments?"

"I think so. Larry's a good guy. We've been buddies for several years now. I pay him by cutting grass and doing odd jobs he needs done. By the way, is there anything I can do to help pay you? I can wash and polish cars."

"That isn't necessary. Social Services arranged for Medicaid to pay your doctor and hospital bills while you need help. From what I'm learning about you, I don't expect you'll need assistance for long."

"Thanks, Doc. It's good of you to say that. I'm not a praying man, but lately I've been praying for my wife and for a better future for my kids."

With a lump in my throat, I nodded. "I'll add you to my prayer list also."

Tears glistened in his eyes, but he quickly blinked them away and nodded his thanks.

"Now, tell me how you're doing physically. Do you have any more cough or shortness of breath?"

"No, not really. I'm a little weak still. Have to rest more often while doing yard work, but okay otherwise."

"Slip your shirt off and have a seat on the examination table so I can have a listen to your breathing." For the next few minutes, I carefully listened to his heart and lungs, and hearing no abnormalities, I looked up and smiled. "I believe you've nearly made a full recovery. Just be careful and don't over-exert yourself yet. Be sure to pace yourself while you work."

"Will do. And thanks for everything, Doc."

I waited as he buttoned his shirt and adjusted his belt. He made eye contact with me, shook my hand, and smiled, then headed for the waiting room to retrieve his children and make another appointment for them to continue their course of vaccinations.

Christine carried Jimmy to the car while Michael's friend, Larry, helped the other children into the backseat. Donna and Christine waved as they drove off with the vehicle once more belching smoke as they left.

Christine turned to me with a guilty look on her face. "Thanks for helping them. My heart really goes out to those poor kids. I hope you don't mind. I told them to come back in a month."

"Well, sure. That's right. What are you sorry about?"

She grabbed her purse and hurried out the door, turning only briefly to answer, "I told them to come at six again." Outside, she jumped in her car, gunned the engine, and took off, spraying gravel against the building.

Donna bent over laughing as I checked my watch. Now 7:10 p.m.

"Oh well."

CHAPTER 6

The next few months passed rapidly as the initially warm, golden days of fall faded with the falling leaves, replaced by a cold, barren, windswept landscape. The first snowfall blanketed the ground in November, hiding the dull browns and yellows of dormant pasture lands. Farmers fed their animals with hay stored in picturesque barns as nature went into hibernation for the short days and long nights of winter cold.

Thursday, December 18, 1974, arrived with bitter cold and blowing snow. Only one week before Christmas and the gifts of candy, cookies, and cards were piling up in the office. Not to be outdone by the patients, we had our own stash of treats to hand out during the week before Christmas. The ladies had Scotch-taped greeting cards all around the reception window, all over the door to the break room, and all down the back hallway. A six-foot-tall artificial fir tree graced the far corner of the waiting room, complete with twinkling lights, sparkling holiday bulbs, and small silver bells hanging from the circling strands of red and gold garland.

Christine had just unlocked the front door for our first patients when sleet began pelleting the window panes and blowing in the doorway as people paused to stomp and shake off snow and ice from their boots. We were glad to be inside out of the storm, listening to soft music as a DJ from the radio station in Glen Falls played two hours of nonstop Christmas and holiday songs on WHCR. Donna placed the radio by the reception window so everyone could enjoy the music.

OB day that week had been conducted on Tuesday as usual, but the first patient Donna placed in a room today was Katy Mills, accompanied by her mother.

Following the usual vital signs and recording of her chief complaint, Donna hurried to the break room.

I set my coffee cup down as she entered. "What are you so excited about this morning?"

"I think Katy is in labor. She's been having contractions all night. They were about every ten minutes and mild with little or no pain at first."

"Like Braxton-Hicks contractions?"

"Yes, just signs of early activity, but at seven this morning, they became painful and closer together, about every four to six minutes. She's also had a little bleeding with mucus. I've got her set up for a pelvic examination."

"No history of ruptured membranes yet?"

"No. They want to know if she's in real labor and needs to go to the hospital."

"And you're just a casual observer with only a scientific interest?"

"Doc, you know I'm dying to know too. So please don't keep us waiting." She headed back to the room.

I had to smile as she hurried down the hall. Donna and Christine were nearly beside themselves with anticipation every time a new baby was due. They made our patients feel as if we were all one big family, adding immeasurably to the medical practice.

I knocked on the door to exam room 1, and Donna cracked the door to be certain it was me before opening it. "She's all ready for you to check."

"Good morning, Katy. This sounds like it could be the real thing. Please tell me all about your symptoms."

"I hope so." She paused to glance toward her mother. "At least Mom thinks it's probably my time to have the baby." After she recounted the symptoms, she showed me a paper with the timing of the contractions, both the frequency and the duration of each one, along with when they became painful. She had just finished going over her record when a particularly hard contraction caused her to catch her breath, then emit a soft groan.

Katy was lying recumbent on the table, and stepping to her side, I palpated the abdomen as it indeed tightened into a moderately strong contraction. It lasted thirty-five seconds and was of good quality.

After it subsided, I nodded at Donna. "We'd better check her before the next contraction starts."

"Right. I checked the fetal heart beat at 150 and the contractions every five to six minutes." Donna smiled and helped Katy slide down toward the end of the table before placing her feet in the stirrups.

I performed a quick bimanual examination, then removed my gloves and looked up at Katy. "I believe you'll have this baby today. You're dilated to four centimeters. The baby's head is well down in the pelvis and the membranes are bulging. The contraction I felt was of moderate strength, but they will get stronger as labor progresses. You aren't going to wait for Christmas."

Mrs. Harrison stood up to assist Katy and was all smiles as I turned to her. "I think you and Katy should get her suitcase and head to the hospital. I'll see you there later. Since this is a first baby, it will probably be a few hours, but she's definitely in early labor and the timing of delivery is difficult to estimate accurately. Her labor will probably strengthen after the membranes rupture."

After Katy left, the day proceeded uneventfully with the usual colds, flu symptoms, and sore throats, all common during Indiana winters. About ninety minutes later, the hospital operator placed a call to the office, which I took in the break room. "Dr. Matlock, please hold for OB."

Within moments, Emily Jarret's voice came over the line. "Dr. Matlock, we have your patient, Katy Mills, P0G1, admitted to the labor and delivery floor. She's dilated at five centimeters and having moderate contractions every five minutes, membranes still intact but definitely in labor. The fetal heart beat remains strong in the 150 to 160 range. I've instituted your routine orders, and I'm guessing it'll be a few hours at least before we need you. I'll keep you informed of her progress. Any further orders?"

"No further orders, Emily. I appreciate your help as usual. I'll be seeing patients in the office until you need me to come in."

"I'll call when we need you. You can count on it, Doctor. Thank you and goodbye."

I smiled, placing the receiver back on the hook. Tall, thin, and dignified, Emily was a head OB nurse with years of experience in labor and delivery. She could write the book on the whole process. Her demeanor was always professional, and she was methodical, proud, and obsessed with the need to run a smooth service. I was glad she was on duty.

Turning to go back to work, I nearly ran into Christine. Her face flushed and she looked like a child caught with her hand in the cookie jar. "Were you eavesdropping on the conversation?" I assumed a disapproving look, trying not to laugh.

Her voice sounded small as she squeaked, "Yes, sorry." She cleared her throat, then continued. "But since you caught me anyway, please refresh my memory. What does P0G1 mean?"

I had to laugh. She looked so embarrassed but was still so inquisitive. "You're too much, Christine. You know what they say about curiosity and the cat."

She pouched out her lower lip. "I know, and I expect to die. But I still want to know. I need to know all the medical terms I can learn so I can do a better job working for you."

I held up my hands. "Okay, okay. I give up. Please write this down so we don't need to go over it again."

She pulled out the pencil that was wedged above her ear and showed me the tablet in her other hand. "Oh, I will. In fact, I'm dying to do just that. I'm the cat, you know."

"In regard to the term P0G1, P means that her parity or para is zero, hence P0. She has never delivered a living or stillborn baby over twenty weeks gestation in the past. G stands for gravida and G1 means that this is her first pregnancy, regardless of the outcome."

"Thanks, Doc. But I have another question. What if she has twins?"

I had to laugh before replying. "First, she isn't having twins."

"But what if she did? What would you call that?"

"Then she would be P2G1. Two babies delivered and one pregnancy. Get it?"

Christine assumed an angelic look. "Thanks again. I just love working here. I can't wait until we have a P2G1 patient." With that she spun around and sped through the door to the waiting room. A truly lovely young lady, she was also nothing if not a ray of sunshine and comic relief during many a routine, humdrum day.

THE OFFICE RECEIVED periodic updates on Katy during the day, duly noting her blood work, vital signs, and progress of labor. As we prepared to close the office at 5:30, Christine looked distressed.

Concerned, I asked, "Something wrong?"

"Katy hasn't had her baby yet. Now I'll have to wait until tomorrow to learn the details."

Donna finished her chores and prepared to leave. Rolling her eyes, she said, "I need to finish my Christmas shopping, and it'll be a relief to get out of here. For the last hour, Christine has been badgering me to ask you to call and check on Katy's progress. I finally pretended not to hear, but she's hard to ignore."

Christine looked down at her desk, where she was finishing up the book work for the day. "Sorry. I just wanted to know if everything is going well for her or not."

Donna stooped over and gave her a hug. "I know, and I'm anxious for her too. But the workflow can't be interrupted to satisfy our curiosity."

Christine grinned. "I'll try not to be so nosy in the future."

"Hold on a minute, ladies. I'm about to go call for an update. I need to know if it's safe to go home for dinner or if I need to go directly to the hospital."

Christine resumed her normally buoyant mood. "Oh, goodie. I can hardly wait to find out."

Donna just shook her head and smiled.

Within mere minutes, I returned from the break room. "Well, I'm on my way to the hospital. Her membranes just ruptured and she's dilated to eight centimeters and in hard labor now. Emily was just about to call when I telephoned."

Christine bounded up from her desk in the small reception room. "You go right ahead, Doc. I'll be happy to lock up and do the night deposit for you." She was all smiles again.

THE STORM HAD ABATED, and the state highway trucks had done a great job of keeping the interstate open to Glen Falls, so I arrived in a timely manner and made my way to labor and delivery. Mildred Long, evening charge nurse on OB, had relieved Emily. Mildred, equally experienced and competent, was short and rotund but very relaxed in her approach to nursing care.

"How's she doing, Mildred?"

She smiled. "Very well. She's ten centimeters and the baby will soon be here. Katy's pushing now. I was just about to call and make sure you were on the way. Vital signs are all good, and fetal heart sounds are regular at 155." She pushed herself up from her chair and lumbered ahead of me to the labor room, where the medical assistant, Sharon Cunningham, sat with Katy and Robert Mills.

A brief exam revealed that it was time to enter the delivery room.

I turned to Robert. "You're wearing scrubs, and you're welcome to accompany Katy while she delivers your baby. Just take a seat at the head of the table. If for any reason you feel ill, please step out into the hallway and have a seat there. If you still feel faint, lie down on the floor. We don't have time to care for you if you pass out."

"I'll be okay, Doc. I don't want to let Katy down. If I feel funny, I just won't watch."

I quickly changed into blue scrubs with a surgeons cap to cover my hair and hurried to the delivery suite.

Mildred made her job look deceptively easy as she and Sharon moved Katy to the delivery table, setting everything in order for the imminent birth, while I scrubbed with surgical soap, then donned a sterile gown over my scrubs and then gloves with Mildred's expert help. She never seemed in a hurry but always accomplished more than any two other nurses.

I took a seat at the end of the table in time to assist with delivery of the head, slowly and carefully, to avoid maternal and infant injuries. Katy groaned as she pushed, her face beet red just before the completion of the infant's birth. Everything progressed quickly after that as I suctioned out the nares and was rewarded by loud protests from the newborn even before full expulsion from the birth canal.

It was only after rapid completion of the birth that I looked on with mingled sorrow and pity at the small, struggling baby girl I cradled in my arms. The lower extremities weren't fully developed. A meningomyelocele, the result of a failure of the spinal column to close properly, was present. Being the bearer of bad news is the hardest duty of any physician, and I was briefly at a loss for words.

Katy sensed something was wrong. "Is the baby okay, Doctor?"

"Yes. Well, yes and no. She appears to be quite strong, as you can hear from her loud protests at leaving the warmth and security of the womb. Unfortunately, she has a problem with her back and legs."

Robert stood up to peer over the end of the table. "What kind of problem, Doc?"

"She has what is known as a meningomyelocele on her lower back. That is a big word that means something went wrong during development. Her lower spine didn't close properly. A portion of the spinal cord and its coverings are herniated out onto her back. I'm afraid her legs are affected."

Robert sat back down, pale and sweating a little. "What does that mean about her legs?"

"Robert, Katy, this has to be urgently repaired by a pediatric neurosurgeon. People born with this defect can live a normal lifespan, but she may never be able to walk."

Katy began to weep and shake. She looked up and extended her hands. "May I hold her now? Whatever is wrong, I want her, and we'll do whatever you say to help her, even if she never walks."

Robert was slowly recovering from the shock. "Will she be normal, other than her legs and back?"

I stood to place the baby in Katy's arms, careful to put no pressure against the defect containing nervous tissue. "As far as I can tell. She's normal in all other respects. After Katy holds her a few minutes, I'll examine her more thoroughly, but she needs to be sent to Indianapolis for care. I recommend Riley Hospital for Children where a pediatric neurosurgeon can care for her. They may be able to close the defect, but only time will tell about the use of her legs."

Katy smiled through her tears at the little bundle in her arms as Mildred carefully covered the defect with moistened sterile-saline dressings. Katy looked at me again. "Her name is Mary Elizabeth, named for the women in the story of the birth of Jesus and John the Baptist."

"That's a good name, Katy. And only God knows the potential of little Mary Elizabeth. Let me encourage you. I know a doctor who had a meningomyelocele that had to be repaired. He walks with crutches but is normal in all other respects."

Robert reached over and took my hand in both of his. "Thanks, Doc. I know we'll get through this with your help."

Katy added, "And with God's help."

I nodded, not trusting my voice with further words to these brave young people.

WITHIN A COUPLE OF HOURS, Riley's transport ambulance with a neonatologist aboard had arrived to take Mary Elizabeth Mills to their neonatal intensive care unit. Katy held her once more before they departed for Indianapolis, reluctantly releasing the little bundle to their care.

Bonita Harrison stayed with Katy while Robert left in his car for Riley Hospital, accompanied by his mother and father, Lauren and Jack Mills, and Katy's father, Clayton Harrison.

I stayed to visit with Katy and Bonita in the private room I had arranged for them on the OB floor, wanting to be sure Katy was stable physically and emotionally before leaving the hospital.

Bonita sat at the bedside holding Katy's hand, silent tears flowing down her cheeks as she tried to comfort her daughter. Katy no longer cried but looked so very sad.

"Can I go home in the morning?" she asked. "I need to be with Mary Elizabeth. She's so small and frail with those poor little useless legs. They don't move at all, do they, Doctor?"

"First, she is small, but her birthweight of six pounds and seven ounces is normal. Second, she is in very good hands at Riley Hospital. Third, I want you to stay at least twenty-four hours. We need to know you're stable before discharge home. I would prefer that you stay all day Friday and go home Saturday." She started to interrupt, so I quickly added, "But I will come in tomorrow evening to check on you. Then we'll see."

"If she's able to be released tomorrow, I'll keep her and Robert close by, whether at home or in Riley Hospital," Bonita said. "I'll make sure she minds whatever you tell her to do." She gave Katy's hand a quick squeeze.

Katy smiled at her, then at me. "Thanks for all you've done for me and our baby. Robert and I appreciate it very much."

As I drove home through blowing snow, I thought over all that had happened to the two families, brought together by an unwanted pregnancy, initially angry and fighting among themselves, now concerned with survival of a tiny baby. The birth of a grandchild, even though handicapped by a difficult start in life, had brought them together in a way that nothing else could.

Christmas lights glistened through the haze of the storm, lighting up homes and pushing back the darkness, bringing cheer and hope of the holiday season. I was reminded that two thousand years ago, the birth of another apparently helpless baby to a young mother had changed the world indelibly. Each precious gift of a newborn child reminds me of the greatest gift ever given to mankind.

CHAPTER 7

"How very sad. I hurt for those young parents." Christine couldn't get over the news the next day in the office. "Why did this happen to the poor little thing?"

"I really don't have an answer for you. There's no family history of neural tube defects."

"What's a neural tube defect?"

"It's a deficiency in the development of the spinal column or skull. Most cases involve the spinal column in varying degrees of severity. For some reason, there is a failed closure of the spine with herniated neural tissue possibly developing. In the worst cases affecting the spine, paraplegia, or paralysis of the lower extremities, can be the result. As to cause, it's likely multifactorial, perhaps a deficiency of some of the B vitamins, cigarette smoke, et cetera. In her case, she took her vitamins, doesn't smoke, and has no known hereditary factors. It can just happen spontaneously by a mutation during development, and we may never know what caused little Mary Elizabeth to develop this problem."

Donna had finished putting the first patients in rooms and joined us in the break room. "We'd like to do something for the family for Christmas. Do you have any ideas what they might need?"

"You ladies are probably better than me at answering that question."

Christine nodded. "How about baby clothes? Do they have enough for her when she's released from the hospital?"

"I know some of the ladies who attend their church. Why don't we call and find out if they know? Last week when I was checking them in, someone mentioned a baby shower for Katy. I don't think they've had the shower yet."

"That's a great idea." Christine had regained some of her usual exuberance. "I'll get on the phone and make inquiries right away."

The ladies returned to the front office, conversing excitedly about a Christmas surprise for little Mary Elizabeth and her family, while I made my way to exam room 1 to see the first patient. Once again, I was thankful for a caring staff and a town with a heart for others. I knew an outpouring of support would be forthcoming.

BY THE CLOSE of the day, Christine and Donna had a list of donations planned by people of the town. Everyone knew about the baby. In a small rural farm town in the 1970s, there were very few secrets. Privacy issues were nearly nonexistent. Hospital admissions and discharges, along with births and deaths, were read over the air daily from the radio station in Glen Falls. Patients could ask to have information withheld, but few ever did.

After locking up for the day, the ladies departed, still excited about their project. I sat alone finishing up charts in the break room when my beeper sounded a loud alarm, my signal to call the hospital operator. I took the last charts to the front and placed them on Christine's desk to file next week. We wouldn't be working tomorrow morning as we usually did on Saturdays since I had given them the day off for Christmas shopping. I needed time to shop for my family as well.

I sat down at the reception desk in the darkened room and picked up the phone to dial the hospital. Illumination from the street lights beaming in the windows provided adequate light for me to see. In those days, beepers were quite limited. Mine only gave a warning sound, alerting me to call the switchboard operator at the hospital. I had no other call system available in those days.

After dialing the number, I leaned back in the chair to watch the snow swirling silently past the window pane.

Rose Adams's voice came over the line. "Memorial Hospital, Rose speaking. May I help you?"

"Hello, Rose. This is Dr. Matlock. You paged me."

"Yes, Dr. Matlock. ER wants to speak with you. Please hold while I transfer your call."

Within moments, Ann Kilgore answered in the ER. "Hello, Doc. Can you hold a moment? Dr. Neal would like to speak with you about a patient."

"Sure. Do you know the name of the patient?"

"Yes, but here he is now. I'll let him tell you about it."

"Dr. Neal here. Dr. Matlock?"

"Yes, what do you have for me, John?"

"I know you're not on call, but we have a request for you to be the admitting doctor. The patient's name is Marilyn Richardson. Her husband is Michael. You take care of the rest of the family, I believe."

"That's correct. What's the problem?"

"You may know the story from the husband. She's been abusing narcotics and took an overdose of heroin tonight. She's awake after a dose of Narcan to reverse it, but she came in comatose. And that's not the worst of it. She's been shooting up. There are track marks all over her arms and legs, and she apparently has hepatitis B. Her liver enzymes are off the chart and she's as yellow as a pumpkin from jaundice. She's also in early liver failure with moderate ascites and peripheral edema of the lower extremities."

"I don't mind taking care of her, but don't you think she should be sent on to Indiana University Hospital if she's that sick?"

"That's just the problem, she's refusing transfer. She's wide awake and appears competent. The only option she'll consent to is admission here overnight."

"Is her ammonia level high?"

"Yes, but it's only fifty, with the upper normal for our lab being thirty-five, so not enough to say she's incompetent."

"Okay. Go ahead and admit her to my service. Do you think she'll even stay the night?"

"That's anybody's guess, Doc. She's not exactly a model citizen."

"Tell her that I'll be in later to see her. I need to go home and eat first, and I'd at least like to see her before she decides to sign herself out, if she does. If her husband, Michael, is there, see if he'll stay with her until I get there. It'll probably be at least an hour and a half."

"Just a second. I'll check with him now." Within moments, Dr. Neal returned to the phone. "He says to take your time. He'll be here. He has kids with him, but Jan Hart just got off work and is taking them home with her. I guess they're neighbors."

"That's right. She knows them well. Okay, go ahead with the admission."

I replaced the receiver on the phone cradle. So much for a quiet evening at home.

TWO HOURS LATER, I sat in the hospital room with Marilyn and Richard, uncomfortable in my sterile mask, gloves, and gown, but ready to examine my newest patient. Deeply jaundiced, body habitus thin except for swollen legs and abdomen, she gazed apathetically at the ceiling directly above her bed. Michael sat in a corner, similarly gowned, masked, and gloved.

"Marilyn, I know we've met briefly before, but hopefully we can become better acquainted as I work with you to help you recover and improve your health. Can you tell me how long you've been ill?"

An uncomfortably long silence ensued, and I had just started to repeat the question when she cut me off abruptly.

"I heard what you said. I'm just thinking how to answer. I'm not sure what you mean by 'sick.' Are you speaking about my need for medication for my nervous condition, or are you talking about hepatitis?"

Nonplussed, I hesitated before responding. "Well, both of course. I believe the problems are related. Don't you?"

She turned her head toward the wall. "Maybe, maybe not. What's it to you?"

"If I'm going to help you, we need to be able to discuss everything related to your medical condition. I'm not trying to interfere in your personal life, other than to assess risk factors with you."

She glared at me. "You want to take away my nerve medication, don't you?"

"What nerve medication are you talking about?"

"The medicine I get from my friends on the street. I need it to survive." She looked at Michael, sitting in the corner with his head down. "He's no help. Lost his job. No money for me to spend on myself. I'm tired of everything about him, and I'm tired of talking with you. If you don't mind, please get lost. I'm going home tonight." She sat up in bed, swung her legs over the side, cursing and swearing, then refusing all help from Michael as he leaped up and hastened to her side. She refused to answer any more questions and demanded her clothing.

I nodded at Michael and left the room. There wasn't anything else I could do without her permission. At the nurses' station, I asked for an AMA (against medical advice) form for her to sign, if she would.

Ann Kilgore looked up in surprise as I approached the desk, having peeled off the gown, gloves, and mask when she exited the room. "That was quick. What happened?"

"Marilyn is totally unreasonable. I can't even talk to her. She's down there berating her husband as if it's his fault she's in here. If he hadn't called for help when her 'friends' dropped her off on her front porch in a nearly comatose condition, she'd probably be dead by now. She ordered me out and is cursing everything and everyone. We need to see if we can get her to sign an AMA form."

Ann shook her head, a look of disgust on her face. "I figured this would happen. She's lost all ability to reason about anything but her need for another quick fix."

"True, but she appears to be competent. I don't think I can keep her or send her to a psych ward against her will."

"No, Doc. She makes bad choices, probably lethal choices, but she knows what she's doing. I've seen her too many times in the ER to believe anything else."

We started back to the room with the AMA papers, and as I carefully formulated what I was going to say to persuade her to stay for care, she nearly ran over us exiting the doorway, refusing to let Michael help her, still angry and cursing. We temporarily blocked her path, and she began screaming at us as she noticed the papers in my hand.

"I ain't signin' nothin'. Get out of the way or I'll spit on both of you." She began chewing as if accumulating saliva, and we backed away.

She brushed past us and spat on the floor instead. Michael hurried after her, took her arm in an attempt to help, and she shook him off, still raging and swearing. "I'd be okay if they hadn't shoved that IV in me to counteract my medicine. You get out of the way and out of my life. I hope I never see you again." With that, she hurried to the elevator, pushed the down button, and was soon on her way out of the hospital, on her own, playing the odds.

I turned to Michael. "I'm so sorry. I don't know what to do or say to help."

Ann put her arm around him as he lowered his head and stood quietly sobbing. "Sit down with me in the nurses' station. I'm going to have a late supper brought up for you. This isn't your fault. You did your best to get help for her. Now it's all up to Marilyn whether she gets help or continues her reckless lifestyle."

While Ann did her best to provide a measure of comfort for Michael, I made my way to the dictation room, where I dictated an extensive note regarding what had transpired. Marilyn was high risk, and everything had to be well documented. As I sat dictating, I pondered calling the police to apprehend her for her own good, but they wouldn't want to get involved unless she had broken a law they could document. I'd been down that road before. I couldn't really blame the police. They were subject to litigation regarding unlawful arrest. Marilyn could deny taking illegal drugs, and it would be hard for them to prove after the fact. There was no good solution.

After finishing my dictation, I checked on a couple of other patients, then returned to see if I could do anything else for Michael. Ann was house supervisor for the evening shift, and she still sat at the desk in the nurses' station filling out the forms she was required to complete for an AMA. She had been a witness to the shocking display of rage as Marilyn left the hospital.

"Where's Michael?"

"He went home, Doc. I've never felt so sorry for anyone in my life. Jan Hart has his kids tonight. She said she could see it coming. In the summer, she can hear Marilyn throwing and breaking things, cursing when he doesn't bring home enough money. It's tragic for those poor children and for him. I believe he still loves her, but obviously the love isn't returned."

"So sad, and it seems even worse this time of year when people should be happy, sharing family time together, and enjoying the holidays. There's a lot of sadness and heartache in our world tonight."

"You're right about that. People like Marilyn have forgotten the reason for the season, as they say."

I nodded, my heart too full of sorrow to respond. I turned to walk to the stairwell leading to the doctors' parking lot.

"Good night, Doc!" Ann called after me. "Thanks for your help. You did your best."

"Thank you, Ann. Please thank the staff for their assistance also."

Is there anything else I could have done? I wondered. A bad feeling about Marilyn Richardson came over me. I hoped I wouldn't be reading about her in the newspaper. Christmas should be a happy time of rejoicing, but it could only be what people made it.

The snowfall had stopped by the time I stood beside my car. Looking up, I saw the clouds had dissipated, leaving a clear sky with distant stars twinkling in the night. That reminded me that many people who met the Great Physician had rejected his help as well. Gazing momentarily at the silent heavens, I felt a unique nearness to the One who had ministered to others so long ago. I no longer felt lonely as I got in my car, turned the ignition, and heard "Silent Night" softly playing on the radio.

The telephone jangling by the head of the bed awakened me in the

60

middle of the night. As I retrieved it from the nightstand, I managed a sleepy, "Hello."

"Dr. Matlock, this is John Neal in the ER. Sorry to awaken you, but I needed to let you know about Marilyn Richardson. I heard what happened, and I'm sorry."

Fully awake now, I asked, "Is she back?"

My heart skipped a beat at the long silence on the phone.

"Yes, she's back. This time she didn't make it. She OD'd on heroin again and left a suicide note. A passing driver saw her body on the sidewalk downtown. It seems her friends supplied her with more of her 'medicine.' It's a crime, but I don't know anything you or I can do about it."

I was up on the side of the bed now. "What about her husband, Michael? Does he know?"

"He knows. He's here with me in the ER now. He said to tell you that he doesn't blame any of us. Marilyn had her chance and made her choices."

"Tell him I'll be right there if he'll wait."

"Sure thing. I believe he'd appreciate that a lot."

Sleep was out of the question as I hurriedly dressed, informed my wife that I was returning to the hospital, and raced through the deserted streets at 3:00 a.m.

After arriving at the hospital, I sat with Michael in the hospital chapel as he wept. There was nothing to say, only grief to share with this man I had come to appreciate.

EARLY MONDAY MORNING, I stood shivering, buffeted by the wind, in the cemetery at Glen Falls as Marilyn's casket was lowered into the ground. My wife, Janet, accompanied me along with Christine and Donna. Office hours had been delayed. Jan Hart held little Jimmy as the older children huddled beside their father. Reverend White offici- ated, and a few people from the hospital along with some of Michael's friends stood beside us. The bitter cold wind flapped the thin tent walls with a vengeance as yet another winter storm approached our county.

It was one of the saddest days in my early practice. We all felt an enormous loss as the service concluded and we exited the cemetery.

CHAPTER 8

I was making late rounds on Tuesday, December 23, when I was again paged for ER. I picked up the phone on the OB floor, where I had just released a mother and baby home to a warm and caring family. She wanted to go home before Christmas Eve, so I was here late in the day to oblige the family.

Ann Kilgore's voice came over the line. "Dr. Matlock, we have one of your patients here and he's asking if you could see him."

"Who is it?"

"Michael Richardson."

After a moment of hesitation, I said, "I'll be down shortly. What's going on with Michael? Nothing serious, I hope."

"He has something in his right eye and seems in a lot of pain."

"That poor man sure has had more than his share of trouble and heartache. Does the injury appear serious?"

"I don't think it's serious, but you'll have to decide when you see him. I believe it's just a foreign body in the eye."

"Okay, see you in a couple of minutes." I sighed and shook my head.

Life just didn't seem fair sometimes. Michael and his family had lost so much in the last few days.

~

On entering the ER, I was surprised to see Art McKay and his crew bringing in another patient. "Hello, Art. Looks like you're working late too."

Art smiled. "We sure are. The snow and ice are making roads and walks treacherous tonight. We brought in one of Doc Langley's patients. She had a fall on the ice in her drive. Appears to have a fractured left hip. What are you up to tonight, Doc?"

Art was the county coroner, so I asked, "Remember the young woman who died of a heroin OD last week?"

"Yes. That was such a shame. Left a young family and husband behind, I believe."

"Unfortunately, he's here with an eye injury. I just finished late rounds, so here I am again."

Art took on a look of concern. "Is there anything I can do to help? I remember now how the husband grieved as we talked. They had little children, didn't they?" Art McKay was a small man as measured in height, but he had a heart as big as all outdoors.

I nodded. "There might be. If you're still here after I see him, I'll let you know."

He nodded. "You do that, Doc. I'll make a point to still be here."

I turned to find Ann Kilgore holding little Jimmy Richardson while one of the orderlies, Wyatt O'Donald, entertained four-year-old Howie and seven-year-old Wendy. He sat in a corner with Howie on his lap and Wendy standing at his side as he read Christmas stories from a holiday book for children. The other nurse and medical assistants were busy admitting Dr. Langley's patient.

Ann smiled. "Say hello to Jimmy, Dr. Matlock. He's being a very good boy."

I tousled the little fella's hair. "Hi, Jimmy. How are you tonight?"

Jimmy tucked his head, shyly laying it on Ann's shoulder.

"Looks like you have a friend."

She nodded. "He's a sweet little child."

"Which room is Michael in?"

"He's in the eye room. Call if you need help."

MICHAEL RICHARDSON SAT HUNCHED over with his right hand holding a moistened white washcloth gently over his right eye. I couldn't help noticing his green summer jacket with ripped-out pocket corners; his faded blue jeans that had seen better days; and his scuffed, run-down-at-the-heels, once-black shoes that had leaked melting snow all over the floor. The right shoe was missing a shoestring and had been laced up with a piece of ordinary white string. He was the picture of abject misery.

"Hello, Michael. What happened to your eye?"

He laid the washcloth down and squinted up at me. "Sorry to bother you, Doc. I guess I'm a lot of trouble." He paused a long moment. "I got sawdust in my right eye, I think. I was rummaging in the trash can at the sawmill for a block of wood. When I held it up to see it better by the streetlight, sawdust or dirt blew in my right eye. I dropped the block, which then struck my face and eye too. Bad luck, huh?"

"You've had your share, for sure. If you don't mind telling me, why were you looking for a block of wood?"

He leaned over with his head down, put the washcloth back over his right eye, and attempted to hide the tears trickling from his eyes. He couldn't trust himself to speak at the time, so I retrieved the eye tray with the topical anesthetic, tetracaine ophthalmic solution, and other eye medications to relieve his pain and better examine the eye.

"Michael, if you can look up at the ceiling, I'll hold your eyelids open for you and numb your eye. It'll sting briefly but then will feel much better in a hurry."

"Okay, but first I'll try to answer your question. It seems a foolish thing for a grown man to be digging through the trash behind the lumber company, but my kids don't have any Christmas gifts."

I gently pried his right eyelids open and quickly instilled the drops. He flinched only slightly with the initial burning sensation, but soon got relief. "I'll give that another minute to work, then I'll have a look with my flashlight and the slit lamp. But I don't understand what you were doing."

Michael took a deep breath. "I hocked my winter coat and boots today at the pawn shop to buy presents for my kids. They've lost so much. I couldn't bear to give them nothing for Christmas. It's not their fault, although I think my oldest thinks it's somehow her fault. I've tried to reassure her, but I don't really know how little girls think."

"I think I know what you mean. Go on."

"I bought them a used play village set, but some of the houses were broken. I fixed them with Elmer's glue, but the little model of a church was damaged beyond repair. I planned to make a church and hospital model with the blocks for the set. That's why I wanted the blocks of wood."

Now it was a while before I could speak. Finally I managed to say, "You can do that?"

He looked puzzled.

"I mean, you can make miniature models of buildings and towns?"

"Oh, sure, it's easy. Woodworking was my hobby when I had a full-time job. I loved making things for the kids. I can use any kind of tool. Remember, I was a maintenance man. Now I'm just a handyman." He looked down at the floor again. "Unfortunately, Marilyn sold all their toys to buy drugs and alcohol. She even sold some of my best tools. The two older ones only have a few broken toys left to play with." He looked back up at me. " I did buy a nice rubber ball for the baby."

I completed the examination and determined that he had nothing worse than a foreign body that I easily removed with a moist cotton applicator. Further examination disclosed a superficial abrasion, easily seen with the slit lamp. After applying a couple more tetracaine drops and antibiotic ointment, I patched his eye. "Okay, Michael. That does it. I need to take another look at your eye tomorrow. I'll be in the office until one on Christmas Eve. Do you think you could get there?"

He shook his head. "Sorry, Doc. I still don't have a way to your office."

"Okay. Tell you what. I'll be making rounds between seven and eight thirty tomorrow. Could you come back to the ER around eight in the morning?"

"That'll work for me okay, but I don't want to take up your time."

"Abrasions usually heal very fast. It won't take long at all to have another look with the slit lamp. Okay?"

"Okay. I'll be here. Thanks for helping me. I'll get you paid in full someday. If there's any work you'd like me to do, I'd be glad to try to work off my debt for all you've done for me and my family."

"Maybe next summer. We'll see. Right now, be careful getting home. I understand the snowstorm is getting worse."

SITTING at the small desk beside the nursing station, I was finishing the ER record when Art approached again. I looked up and smiled. "Are you and your crew about finished?"

"We're about ready to go back to Glen Oaks. I still want to know if there's anything we can do to help the Richardson family."

Ann Kilgore interrupted our conversation when she nudged Art and pointed at the ER exit. Michael and his three children were just leaving the hospital. Little Jimmy nestled in Michael's left arm while the other two stayed close beside them as icy wind gusts with stinging pellets of mixed sleet and snow blew into the ER as the automatic doors swung open.

Michael bent into the wind, an old sock hat pulled down over his ears, as he did his best to shield Jimmy from the wind and snow. Wendy held tightly to her father's right hand as she clutched Howie's smaller hand in her left. The children had on old coats and mittens, but Michael lacked even gloves for protection from the cold. He wore the collar of his old jacket turned up in a vain attempt to keep snow from falling down his neck onto his shirt.

The swirling snow quickly buried their tracks as they trudged into the night, wading through at least eight inches of snow that had already fallen. The outdoor ER lights revealed the family for only a few seconds before they vanished in a sudden whiteout of blinding snowfall.

I looked at Ann. "Don't they have a ride?"

She shook her head and sighed. "No, his friend brought them but had to go on to his job."

Obviously disturbed, Art started for the door. "Maybe I can catch them. We'd be glad to take them home." He also disappeared into the storm briefly before returning, covered with snow and shivering with the cold. "The snow's coming down so fast I couldn't even see which way they went. I tell you, Doc, we have to do something."

"I'm game. What do you have in mind? No one should have to spend Christmas like that poor family."

Ann and Wyatt had also joined us, equally interested in providing assistance.

"We have a project going for Katy and Robert Mills already," Art said. "Plenty of money and gifts have come in for them. We just have to expand what we're doing to include another family this year. I don't care what town they're from."

Ann and Wyatt nodded. Ann lived in Glen Oaks and knew the family well. Wyatt was familiar with the birth of the Mills baby with congenital spinal defect, as were all the hospital employees.

"We have considerable money left to spend from donations from the hospital employees," Wyatt said. "I'm the chairman of the Christmas gift committee. I'm sure I'll have no problem getting the Richardson family added on as a needy family to help."

"My office will help," I added. "Christine and Donna will want to be included. They care very much for all our patients, especially those who are most needy."

ABOUT AN HOUR LATER, I carefully drove back to Glen Oaks through the quiet whiteness of the countryside. The precipitation had finally tapered to flurries after dumping nine inches of fresh snowfall. The county snowplows had not yet started clearing the roads, which remained slick and treacherous, but the wind died down as the winter storm blew off to the northeast. The first stars were just twinkling faintly as the overcast sky gave way to scattered clouds.

The thermometer dropped precipitously as I made my way home to a late supper with my family, but I still reveled in the knowledge of the wonderful people I worked with in the communities of Glen Oaks and Glen Falls.

CHAPTER 9

*W*ednesday dawned clear and cold with temperatures in the low single digits. The bright morning sun just cresting the eastern horizon shone down on the sparkling white landscape as I arrived at the office in Glen Oaks.

I doffed my coat and hat upon entering the warm break room. Christine had just turned on the coffee pot, which permeated the air with the aromatic scent of fresh coffee. "Merry Christmas, Christine. It's a beautiful day despite the cold."

"Merry Christmas to you too, Doc. I can hardly wait to begin delivering our gifts when we finish working today."

Donna arrived, tugging off her coat and scarf. "Merry Christmas, everybody. It's certainly a beautiful Christmasy day. I'm glad you called us last night about the Richardson family. Christine and I plan to pick up gifts at Barry House's general store right after we finish, hopefully by one. I called Art this morning. He's going to borrow the Glen Oaks Community Church bus to deliver packages to the needy families on the list, starting about four o'clock. If it's all right, we'll come back here to wrap the gifts this afternoon. That'll save us the time of having to return home first. The list includes the Millses and the Richardsons. Art invited Christine and me to join them on the bus. A number of the young people from the church are going along to help distribute the gifts and to sing Christmas carols. It'll be a great time together."

Christine clapped her hands. "What fun! What a great way to celebrate Christmas! Will you come along, Doc?"

"No, I have to return to the hospital. A couple of the patients want to be discharged this afternoon. If their labs are okay, I promised to release them in time for their family celebrations. Besides, my family has plans for this evening too. I miss a lot of family time anyway, and I don't want to disappoint my wife and children."

The morning flew by as patients came in for appointments just before the long holiday weekend. We planned to take off on Christmas Day, Thursday, and remain off until the following Monday, December 29. Cookies, candy, nuts, cakes, and other goodies continued to fill up the table in the break room as friends and neighbors continued to bless us with an outpouring of holiday cheer.

Finally, Donna closed and locked the door after the last patient departed. "Whew. It's one fifteen. Not bad for a holiday. We almost finished on time."

"Ladies, you have to help me before you take off."

Christine looked concerned. "Really?"

"Yes, really. I need you to take whatever you want of the holiday treats. Keep some for yourselves and give the rest to the people you deliver gifts to this afternoon. Above all, have a good time and a wonderful Christmas."

Christine was all smiles again. "Thanks for the Christmas bonus. It'll come in handy."

"Yes, thank you for the generous bonus," Donna chimed in. "Now, we have a little surprise for you."

"Oh, you do?"

Christine retrieved a package from beneath the reception counter. "From Donna and me. Merry Christmas."

They waited expectantly as I opened my office gift, a beautiful winter landscape of a snow-covered frozen pond in the foreground with a thick stand of fir trees in the background. It was a beautiful work of art, one my wife and I would enjoy for many years.

"Thank you, ladies. I didn't expect this, but I do appreciate your thoughtfulness. You both do a great job, working hard and caring for our patients all year long. I trust you'll both be able to spend time with your families during the holiday."

They quickly donned their coats, boots, and scarves, talking animatedly as they hurried off for one last round of Christmas shopping at House's general store.

I locked up and hurriedly made my way to the hospital to discharge some anxious patients if it appeared safe for their release. I looked forward to an evening at home with my own family afterward.

CHRISTMAS MORNING ARRIVED with overcast skies and lazy snowflakes cascading to the ground. It was altogether beautiful to behold as I drove to the hospital to make early morning rounds. I only had three patients still on my census, and one of them would be going home with family.

I started on the medicine floor and was surprised to see Art McKay with his crew already there. "Merry Christmas, Art. Did you bring in someone this morning?"

"No, we're picking up a patient to return to the nursing home. Nothing else on the schedule, at least not yet."

"How did things go last night? Did many of the young people go with you?"

"It was beautiful, Doc. We had twenty-eight including your office girls. We delivered all the gifts and then went to the church parsonage to have coffee, hot chocolate, and Christmas cookies and cupcakes."

"I know you had several on your list, but how did it go with our two needy families?"

Art beamed. "Let me tell you about it."

ROBERT AND KATY had returned home for a little rest at the urging of their families. Both were exhausted from the long drives to Indianapolis, forty-five miles one way, and the seemingly endless hours in the hospital with baby Mary Elizabeth, who was slowly recovering from major surgery to close the spinal defect. They were still living in an upstairs apartment in Glen Oaks, but failed to hear the feet of the carolers trooping up the wooden stairway.

Katy was warming up dinner while Robert lounged on the living room couch, glancing at the accumulated newspapers left on the porch over the previous several days. Between working all day and commuting back and forth, he felt totally spent. He had just started reading the sports page about the local high school basketball team when a knock sounded at the door.

"Can you see who that is, honey?" Katy called out from their small kitchenette.

Robert sighed, folded his paper back up, and laid it on the couch. "Okay, dear."

Opening the door, Robert was overwhelmed by the crowd of well-wishers on their stairway and small deck. He stood back and beckoned them in.

They entered singing Christmas carols and bearing gifts, which they stacked under and around the small Christmas tree, nearly hiding it from sight. Katy hurried in, wiping flour on her apron, trying to smooth her dress, and blinking back tears.

Robert kept shaking his head. "I just don't know what to say. This is such a wonderful surprise."

Katy came to his side, shrugged her shoulders, and put her arm around Robert's waist. "We didn't know you were up to this. I'm embarrassed about how I must look, but we weren't expecting company."

I laughed heartily, doffed my Santa Claus hat, and bowed. "Katy, you look just fine with flour in your hair and on your apron. It's very becoming."

She flushed bright red for a few seconds, brushing at her hair and leaning against Robert.

I smiled. "Just kidding, Katy. There's no flour in your hair."

"Oh, you! I'll get even with you for that, Art McKay. Just you wait."

Everyone in the group enjoyed a laugh, then turned to file out, singing "We Wish You A Merry Christmas."

"THAT'S REALLY WONDERFUL, ART," I said. "You really surprised them. How about the Richardsons? Were you able to see them also?"

"We made several stops to leave gifts with needy families, but that was the highlight of the evening. We went there last. Christine and Donna really helped out with that visit especially. They'll no doubt want to tell you all about it next week, but let me fill you in from my standpoint."

~

TRYING NOT to think about the future, Michael sat in the living room in a big old stuffed chair with Jimmy and Howie on his lap while Wendy sat beside him on the arm of the chair. He read to the children from a Christmas storybook from when he was a child. When he came to the part about gifts left under the tree, he choked up and had to stop. In this small home, there was no Christmas tree and only a few used and reconstructed toys for his children.

Wendy seemed to understand and patted his arm. "It's all right, Daddy. We like it when you read to us like this."

He brushed a tear from his eye and was about to resume the story when the doorbell rang. He got up and set the children down in the chair as he went to answer the door. "Yes, can I help you?"

"You sure can, Michael," I said. "You can let me in out of the cold."

Michael was momentarily confused. Then recognition dawned in his eyes. "Oh. You're Mr. McKay, the coroner. Do I need to sign more papers or something?"

I smiled as the group began singing "Hark the Herald Angels Sing" and filed inside. Christine and Donna led the way with armloads of grocery sacks filled with treats for the children, a fully cooked roast chicken that only needed to be warmed, jugs of milk, and a brand-new thermos filled with hot coffee for Michael.

Michael stood speechless, gazing in wonder as the men carried in a partially decorated six-foot Christmas tree and stood it in a corner.

Several young ladies began adding the finishing touches, hanging various ornaments while the children rushed to join them, clapping their hands and laughing.

Wyatt, the orderly from the hospital, had joined the group once we arrived in Glen Falls. I stopped to pick him up at his home, and he was the last to enter, carrying a pair of new winter boots, a brown leather jacket fresh off the shelf of the local department store, and a sack containing several new shirts and socks.

Michael stared in amazement at the growing pile of toys and gifts being placed beneath the tree, shaking his head in wonder. Nothing like this had ever happened to him in the past. He had no clue what to say.

I put my Santa Claus hat on and walked over to give Michael a bear hug. "Merry Christmas, Michael. I believe your luck is about to change."

Michael blinked several times and managed a smile.

Wyatt approached next. Seeing Michael's obvious embarrassment, he said, "I won't give you a bear hug like Art. He always gets carried away. But I will give you this greeting card. Go ahead and open it."

Michael finally found his voice. "I never in my wildest dreams expected anything like this. I wish I had something to give each and every one of you. What awesome people! What awesome friends, for that is what you are."

"What's in your card, Michael?" Donna asked.

"Oh, yeah. I almost forgot in the excitement." He carefully tore open the envelope, read the message about the joys of Christmas, then pulled out a paper with a check carefully folded inside. He read it, reread it, and stood in silence, trying hard not to sob. Finally, he took a deep breath. "It's a check for two hundred dollars from all of you and others at the hospital, and a letter from the hospital maintenance department. I put in my application for a job many months ago, and it contains an offer of a job, starting next week. I can't believe it."

I pounded him on the back while Wyatt pumped his right hand in a vigorous handshake and everyone cheered, even the children. They didn't know exactly what was happening but quickly caught on to the spirit of joy and thanksgiving.

Finally, the food was stored in the kitchen, the table set for four, the gifts neatly stacked, and the happy carolers on the way out the door. Wyatt was last to leave. He paused to congratulate Michael once more. "Michael, I believe you and I are going to be good friends. Now, I know you don't attend church regularly, because I've heard you mention it in the ER, but I'd like to take you to Christmas morning services at nine tomorrow. There are new clothes for the kids, and dress shirts and slacks for you. Would you honor me by coming as my guest? I live next door to my mom and dad. They heard about you and asked me to invite you and the children for Christmas dinner with us at their home. Will you come?"

Michael nodded, again too overcome for words. Finally, he said, "The children and I are happy to accept your invitation. I need to get them in church. It looks like this is a good time to start. This is a Christmas I'll remember and cherish always, even after such tragedy, loss, and heartbreak. Thank you so much for remembering me and my kids."

Michael followed Wyatt onto the porch. He waved and called after us, "Thank you! Thank all of you for making this a good Christmas for me and my children. Merry Christmas to all."

"That's a beautiful story, Art," I said. "I'm so glad we were able to help both families, and the other needy families as well. That's what the season is all about, giving in memory of One who gave His all."

"Right you are, Doc. Well, Merry Christmas and have a wonderful day with your family."

"You too, Art. You too." I turned down the hall. I had one more task for the morning. Michael had just arrived with his family on their way to the church service, and I was to recheck his eye, but from what I'd been told he was improving and adjusting to his loss. I wanted to see for myself how he was doing and wish him and his family a blessed Christmas.

CHAPTER 10

A blizzard ushered in the new year with snow drifts piling up to first-story roofs in some areas along the highway. For two days, I was snowed in at home. Thankfully, none of my OB patients went into labor during that time. We were unable to reopen the office until Monday, January 6.

Arriving at the office to begin the day, I was relieved to find that one of my patients had cleared our lot with his tractor. I entered through the back door as usual, comforted by the familiar warmth of the break room and the fragrant aroma of fresh-brewed coffee. I removed my snow-covered boots and sat down to put on my dress shoes.

Donna came through the hallway door with a stack of charts. "Good morning and a belated happy New Year."

"Happy New Year to you. Did Christine get here safely?"

"Yes, she's not been able to leave the reception desk to hang up her coat and hat. She just threw them on top of one of the file cabinets. The phone's ringing off the hook. A lot of our patients are still stranded on county roads that haven't been plowed by the highway department. I don't think we'll be too busy today, except for answering the phone, calling in refills, and seeing the few brave souls who dare to venture out in the cold."

"A lot of cancellations?"

"Yes, at least this morning there have been."

"Is anyone here to be seen yet?"

"No, but Robert Mills is on the way. If you can believe it, he just called in this morning and wants a physical examination."

I smiled and shook my head. "People never cease to amaze me. Why in this weather? The temperature is only five above with a wind chill factor of ten below."

"I'm sure I don't know, but Christine said he was very insistent."

I relaxed, holding my favorite cup and savoring the hot coffee as it warmed my hands and body. Swiveling my chair, I watched our neighbor fork hay over the fence to his horses as they waded through one- and two-foot drifts outside the barn door to the paddock where he kept them confined on wintry days.

Our Christmas tree still stood in a far corner since the office had been closed during the New Year's holiday and the latest snowstorm. The ladies would no doubt take it down since it would likely be a slow day due to the storm.

I enjoyed a respite of twenty minutes before the first patient was ready to be seen.

～

I PICKED up the first chart, seeing Donna's note: *Robert Mills for physical exam.*

Upon my entering the room, Robert jumped up to shake my hand. "Good morning. Some weather, huh?"

I nodded. "It's great weather if you like winter cold and snow. You surely don't mind it, coming in for a physical examination. What's up? Are you sick?"

"No, nothing like that. I have to have a form filled out for insurance. The insurance salesman told me to see you to have it completed."

We both sat down and I studied the form. "Life insurance?"

"Yeah, I'm trying to get approved for twenty-five thousand dollars life insurance on myself."

In those days, that was a lot of money for a young man. My curiosity piqued. "You're sure that you're not sick?"

"Nah, Doc, I'm fine. I'm just trying to provide for Katy and the baby, just in case."

"That's very thoughtful of you. How is little Mary Elizabeth doing?"

"She came through her surgery well. The defect in her back was successfully closed. The neurosurgeon said she probably won't ever walk normal, only with a walker or crutches, but she's okay otherwise. The pediatricians at Riley Hospital have been really swell. They ran all kinds of tests on Mary Elizabeth and say that she is completely normal otherwise."

"That's great to hear. Will she be able to come home soon?"

"They think in about three more weeks, maybe even two. We're trying to get all set up. Katy's been at the hospital all through the storm. When we heard the weather report on New Year's Eve, she decided to stay while I came home to get back to work as early as possible."

"The feed mill is probably closed though."

"Yeah, it's closed, but I have other jobs too."

"Really? What are you doing?"

"I'm working for Barry House, delivering medicine to people who are shut-in because of illness, and now those stranded by the weather."

"You'd better be careful out in these freezing temperatures."

He smiled. "You sound just like Katy. She's always worried."

"That's because she loves you, Robert. She's probably worried about you doing two jobs now."

"I know. I don't mind it, really. But I'm not working just two jobs."

I raised my eyebrows, waiting for him to continue.

"Actually, I have three jobs. I'm also making rural newspaper deliveries for the *Glen Falls Daily News*."

"No wonder Katy's worried. What time do you go to work for that job?"

"I get up at three thirty to have a quick breakfast snack and head to Glen Falls to pick up newspapers at four thirty. I'm getting good at my route. I have all the papers delivered by six thirty, just in time to swing by Barry's pharmacy and see if there are any urgent deliveries before I start at the feed mill. I have to be at the feed mill at eight Monday through Friday. I've got more time for my newspaper route and drug store deliveries on Saturday, and I'm off to go to church on Sundays."

I sucked in my breath and slowly blew it out. "Wow. No wonder you want life insurance. You're going to be an old man soon enough working like that."

Robert laughed. "I'm pretty strong and healthy now, as far as I know."

"I hope you stay that way, but seriously, you may be doing yourself and your family more harm than good. I'm sure Katy would rather have you than twenty-five thousand dollars. Have you thought about that?"

Robert clasped his hands together and looked at the floor. Several seconds passed before he looked back up and made eye contact. "If you won't tell anybody, I'll tell you why I'm doing this."

I hesitated, perplexed. "Okay, if that's your wish. I'm not in the habit of sharing personal information about my patients anyway, not unless they ask me to. Not even with a spouse, not without permission."

"I know, and I appreciate it. This is a small town, Doc. I just had to be sure."

I waited for him to continue.

"I've made a lot of changes in my life. I'm attending church and got right with the Lord. Since you're a Christian, I know you'll be glad to hear that."

"That's right. I'm happy for you taking that action. You'll never regret it."

"I've been praying a lot about my wife and baby. I'm concerned about them as well. I don't think Katy has really got her life straightened out yet. I want her to find the same peace of mind and soul that I've found in Jesus. I want Mary Elizabeth to be brought up in church."

"Doesn't Katy go to church with you?"

"Yes, she does. But she's what a lot of people call a nominal Christian. She's not made a commitment to be a real Christian."

"How do you know that?"

"I love her, but I live with her. It's not hard to tell."

"How so?"

"She blames God for our baby's handicap. And there are a lot of other little tip-offs to her true state of spirituality."

"And you don't? Blame God, I mean."

"No, we made wrong decisions. It's not God's fault."

"I agree. But you both need to understand that even if you had done everything right, that wouldn't guarantee a normal pregnancy outcome. Don't take on a load of guilt over the baby's condition."

"I know that too. I'm just saying it doesn't help to blame God."

"You've gained a lot of maturity since the birth of your baby." I sensed that something else was troubling Robert, so I waited for him to finish his thoughts.

After another long pause, Robert continued, "I've been counseling with Reverend White. He's a wonderful man of God. He's helped me a lot, but there's one thing I haven't even told him."

"Yes?"

"I'm not going to live very long. I won't be around to help little Mary Elizabeth grow up."

Thoroughly taken aback, I interjected, "How can you possibly know that?"

Robert looked quite sad. "I've dreamed about dying three times in the last week. I go to sleep and have the same dream, or maybe a vision. I see Katy weeping, holding Mary Elizabeth at my casket after Reverend White finishes preaching my funeral service."

I sat in stunned silence, not liking what I heard but not knowing what to say.

Robert must have noticed my dismay. "It's not all bad, Doc. I've had a little glimpse of heaven at the end of every dream. I can't even describe the beauty of what I've seen. My dream always ends the same. A voice says, 'Well done, good and faithful servant.'"

"I don't know what to say, Robert. I don't like for any of my patients to give up and speak about dying."

"Doc, I don't expect you to say anything. Let's just get on with my exam, and remember not to tell anyone about my dreams, at least not while I'm still alive. Afterward? Well, you'll have to be the judge."

Robert's physical exam was completely normal, as I suspected it would be, but I felt a special concern for this precious young man who was doing his best to provide for his family. As he stood up to leave, I shook his hand. "Is there anything else I can do for you today?"

He shook his head. "Nothing I know of, except just pray for me. That's all I ask."

I followed Robert to the waiting room. No one else had arrived yet. As he went out the door, he turned and smiled, waving and merrily saying, "Happy New Year, everybody."

I watched his car carefully pull out onto the slick roadway and drive on until lost to sight.

"What's wrong?" Christine asked from behind the reception desk. "Did he not pass his physical? You look like you've seen a ghost."

I turned. "What did you say?"

"I said you looked like you saw a ghost. Is something bad wrong with Robert?"

"Oh, no, he's quite healthy. He passed his insurance physical." As I walked back to the break room, Christine sat muttering to herself.

Donna returned to the reception area after cleaning up room 1 for the next patient. "What's wrong, Christine?"

"Oh, nothing. Doc looked so distressed when Robert left. He looked like he'd seen a ghost, but he said the physical was normal. I don't get it." Then she raised her voice as she finished, "And I don't like mysteries."

Donna shook her head and chuckled. "Your curiosity is going to get the best of you one of these days."

Christine stuck her tongue out, but the phone rang, ending their banter for the time being.

~

TUESDAY, January 21, OB and newborn day, arrived. The snow remained piled up in fields, yards, and along roads, but the highways and most of the secondary roads were drivable again. We were midway through the morning when pleasantly surprised by the arrival of Robert, Katy, and Mary Elizabeth on the way home from Riley Hospital.

Donna placed them in my office, otherwise known as room 4, and Christine couldn't remain at her desk any longer. She accompanied me to see them after bargaining with Donna to watch the front desk and answer the phone. Christine held Mary Elizabeth while I talked with the parents.

"Well, this is certainly a surprise," I said.

Robert was all smiles. "It's great to have my family home again. I took off work at the feed mill today to go get them from the hospital."

Katy looked at him reproachfully. "I didn't know until today that he's working three jobs. We'll have to talk about that when we get home."

"I advised him against it, but what does a doctor know?" I laughed as Robert grinned at me.

Katy was not pleased. "And we don't need that expensive insurance he just bought. He's young and healthy. There's plenty of time for that later."

Sobered now, Robert just winked at me.

An uncomfortable silence ensued before I spoke up. "To what do we owe the privilege of this visit?"

Katy glared at Robert before answering, "The Riley pediatricians asked that we bring Mary Elizabeth in every other week for a weight check and to see you if she seems to be developing any problems. We have to take her to the outpatient department at Riley every month for the next several months. She lost some weight, which they said is not unusual with her surgery, but they want her watched closely."

"Let's see, her birth weight was ..."

"Six pounds and seven ounces," Robert filled in.

"She lost weight down to five pounds eight ounces," Katy added. "She's back up to six pounds two ounces at release today."

I reviewed the baby's new office chart. Donna had already weighed Mary Elizabeth. "It looks like our scale checks the same here. So we'll just keep close track of that with you."

After exchanging a few more pleasantries, they prepared to leave and Katy turned to me. "Please talk some sense into my husband the next time he comes in to see you. He's working way too hard."

"I know he is. I already tried to discourage him in this, but he's a determined young man. I do appreciate that he's taking fatherhood responsibly, but I hope he'll listen to you and slow down." I shook Robert's hand. "You have a fine family, but take care of yourself too."

"I'll try to be careful."

"Thanks for everything, Doc," she said as she left the room. "We appreciate your good care of us."

Robert nodded in agreement. "Thanks a lot. Goodbye, Doc."

Christine followed them down the hallway, animatedly talking and gesturing.

I watched as they disappeared around the corner, worried by the way Robert had said goodbye to me. That wasn't his usual way of speaking. I shook my head in dismay, but perhaps I was reading more into it than he intended. I certainly hoped so, but I couldn't shake the sense of oppression that settled over me the rest of the day.

CHAPTER 11

ead down, leaning into the wind, Michael trudged through the foggy streets at five fifteen in the morning. The glare of the streetlights illuminated little, only adding to the opaque whiteness of the winter wonderland directly beneath the light poles. A heavy frost gleamed from the utility posts and ornate metal fences along his route. Otherwise, darkness reigned on the streets of Glen Falls. Although chilled and shivering a little, he strode through the darkness with a new confidence. The date was Monday, February 3, the start of his second full month in maintenance at the hospital in Glen Falls.

His boss, Monty Karr, had called him in early to help with an electrical breakdown in one of the surgery suites. Monty had already praised his skill and, unknown to Michael, had advised administration that he had greater ability than the other six men working for him. The others had been employed for between seven to twenty years, but Monty already saw Michael as his likely replacement when he retired.

Michael had bundled the children up early and taken them to stay with Jan Hart. She was his go-to babysitter whenever available, and she was off work the next two days. He glanced up into the darkness and prayed a brief prayer of thankfulness. He wasn't over the needless death of his wife, but he felt that God had led him and his children into a new chapter in their lives. He now attended church with Wyatt and had found a personal relationship with the God of the universe. He had much to be thankful for on that cold, fog-shrouded morning.

He approached a busy intersection and started to step into the street when he saw a car coming from the opposite direction lose control on a patch of icy pavement and begin spinning in a circle, out of control, toward him. With no time to think, Michael dived out of the way, landing hard on his face and scraping his knees on the sidewalk, just beyond where the car came to a terrifying stop against a fire hydrant.

The entire front end of the vehicle had been demolished and water spewed from the broken hydrant, splashing Michael with rapidly freezing water. The engine had been shoved back into the interior of the car, trapping and pinning the driver in place.

Adrenaline surging, Michael jumped up, ran to the driver's-side door, and tried to open it. He could see a young man inside, still conscious but in obvious impending shock. He began screaming, pounding on the door with his bare hands. "Pull the lock up! I'll get you out!"

Smoke billowed from the hood despite the stream of water from the hydrant, and Michael smelled gasoline.

The occupant looked up at Michael and twisted as best he could to pull up the door lock.

Lights were coming on in the houses adjoining the street at the accident site. A neighbor looked out and yelled, "Is anyone hurt?"

"Call an ambulance and the fire department!" Michael screamed back. "There's a man trapped in the wreckage."

Finally, the driver managed to reach across his chest with his right hand and pull up the lock. Michael heard the click of the lock and pulled with all his might on the twisted car door. After what seemed an eternity, the door finally gave and Michael lost his balance, falling back on the sidewalk again. Not realizing that his face, head, and knees were bleeding, he scrambled up and hurried to pull the driver from the wreckage.

The man was still pinned by the bent steering wheel. In desperation, Michael leaned over the driver, pushing against the steering wheel with all his might, careful not to push against the driver, and finally managed to bend the steering wheel column away from the entrapped young man. Flames began to leap from beneath the hood of the wrecked vehicle as Michael desperately pulled the victim from the now-burning car. Flames briefly seared the left side of his face as he finally freed the driver and dragged him to safety in a snow bank in the closest yard. A crowd quickly gathered and assisted in moving the driver a safe distance as the car became engulfed in flames.

Still bleeding profusely from facial and occipital scalp wounds, Michael knelt beside the victim. "Hey! You okay, buddy?"

The young man blinked. "Don't know," he whispered. "Thanks for help. I'm Robert Mills. Please call my wife. Tell her I'm ready."

"I promise, Robert. I'll see she gets the message."

The ambulance crew arrived, lights flashing and sirens blaring. Two EMTs jumped out and moved back the gathering crowd to assess Robert. One of them motioned to the ambulance driver. "Find a place for this other guy to sit down while we attend to the one on the ground."

Michael started to protest, but the driver simply guided him to the side of the ambulance and sat him in the front seat while he applied bandages with pressure to stop multiple areas of hemorrhaging scalp and facial wounds. Michael had struck the back of his head when falling on the sidewalk the second time, and the most profuse bleeding came from deep scalp wounds on the back of his head.

The driver resisted Michael's efforts to push him away, knowing his adrenaline hadn't worn off yet. Used to the irrational reactions of accident victims, the driver ignored him when possible, but finally became frustrated in his attempt to care for Michael. "Look, buddy. You and your friend have been in a serious accident. Just sit still and let me take care of you. My name's Rick. What's your name?"

Michael was still agitated. "I wasn't in the car. I was too close to the accident for comfort, but I'm glad I was there. I pulled that man out before the fire engulfed the whole vehicle. And my name is Michael Richardson. I was on my way to work in the hospital. I work in maintenance there. I was called in early and happened to be walking there when the driver lost control and crashed right beside me."

A fire engine arrived and worked to control the fire and repair the break in the water line. Meanwhile, the first two EMTs wheeled Robert Mills, strapped on a gurney, to the back of the ambulance and loaded him inside. A second ambulance arrived with two more EMTs, and Michael was turned over to their care.

The first ambulance took off with lights flashing and sirens blaring, and Michael was stabilized, also placed on a gurney against his wishes, and whisked off to the hospital. The Glen Falls police were on the scene, helping to secure the crash site and protect onlookers from injury.

I WAS SHAVING when my telephone rang at 6:10 a.m. I stepped into the hallway to pick up the telephone from a small table and heard the voice of Ann Kilgore on the line.

"Dr. Matlock, this is Ann in the ER. We need you to come in right away if you can. We have two of your patients here from a serious accident."

"Sure thing. Who do you have?"

"You know Robert Mills?"

My heart sank. "Yes. Go on, please."

"His car skidded on ice and ran into a fire hydrant. He was trapped inside and it caught on fire. A passerby pulled him out to safety, but he's very critical. Dr. Neal thinks he has a ruptured spleen and maybe a liver laceration. He's in shock and barely conscious. Dr. Hendrick is on his way and will probably need you to scrub in to assist with emergency surgery."

"Okay. You said there were two patients of mine involved in the accident. I hope his wife wasn't with him."

"Oh, no, there wasn't anyone with him. He was by himself, but Michael Richardson was on his way to work early and was injured pulling Robert from the wreckage. He has a number of injuries. I'll explain more when you get here. I've got to go. Dr. Hendrick just got here and needs assistance."

I placed the receiver back on the hook with a feeling of mixed sadness and horror. I could almost hear Robert telling me about seeing his own funeral, just like he had so recently done. I went to the bedroom to notify my wife that I would be skipping breakfast, then hurried to finish getting ready for work.

Sweetheart that she is, she handed me a toasted peanut-butter-and-jelly sandwich as I kissed her goodbye minutes later and rushed out the front door.

~

I ARRIVED at the hospital at 6:50 after a harrowing thirty-minute drive over slick roads. I had practically inhaled the sandwich my wife gave me, washing it down with a cup of milk that she also provided. Leaving my coat and hat in the doctors' lounge, I double-timed to the ER. Dr. Hendrick already had scrubs on and was wheeling an ER cart bearing a pasty-white Robert Mills to the elevator for transport to the surgery suites on the third floor. A unit of blood hung from one of the short IV poles attached to the cart and was infusing into his right arm with a blood pressure cuff around the bag to increase the infusion rate. A liter of normal saline suspended from a pole on the corresponding side was running wide open into his left arm.

Rob glanced at me in passing and called over his shoulder, "Better ride up on the elevator with us. Bill Johnson is already setting up anesthesia in suite two. You can change into scrubs and join us as soon as possible. I'm going to scrub and start as soon as he's ready."

The elevator doors closed as two surgery scrub nurses accompanied us up to the third floor and the OR. The only sound was the rapid beeping of the cardiac monitor accompanied by an occasional low groan from Robert.

Within ten minutes, I had scrubbed in and joined Rob Hendrick, who already had the abdomen open and was suctioning a large pool of blood with a suction catheter. I took the retractors to free up his hands while he continued to suction and packed the wounds with sterile-saline-moistened laparotomy sponges in an attempt to tamponade the bleeding sites.

The circulating nurse removed Rob's fogged eyeglasses and quickly wiped the moisture off before replacing them on his face. Sweat trickled down his forehead and around his mask as he worked feverishly to stop the hemorrhaging.

Bill Johnson monitored his blood pressure as he continued to pour in type-specific blood and infused saline to expand the blood volume. He looked over the head of the table and said, "I can't keep his blood pressure above sixty systolic. Can you see what's bleeding?"

"He has a stellate laceration of the liver and a ruptured spleen," Rob answered. "He must have already lost his total blood volume into the abdomen. Keep the blood coming."

Bill Johnson looked grim. "I'll do what I can. He's had three units of packed red blood cells already and three more are on the way. Normal saline is still running. Are you making any progress?"

Before Rob could answer, the monitor stopped beeping and the EKG complex on the screen went into straight-line mode as a loud alarm sounded. Robert's heart had stopped beating, and the blood flow into the abdomen slowed and ceased.

Bill shook his head. "I think he's gone. Pupils already dilated and nonreactive. What do you want to do now? Are you going to open the chest?"

Rob was already doing just that. He jerked the sterile sheets away from the abdomen and chest wall, made a quick incision along the margin of the left mid-rib cage, inserted rib spreaders handed to him by the circulating nurse, and cranked them open to expose the heart. Bill continued to supply oxygen while Rob incised the pericardium, reached into the bloody pericardial cavity, and began open-chest cardiac massage. He glanced at me. "Large cardiac contusion with pericardial bleeding. I'm afraid it's hopeless."

Bill gave IV epinephrine in a futile attempt to stimulate the heart, but Robert remained in asystole, no heart beat whatsoever, no rhythm to even try cardiac defibrillation with an electrical shock.

Bill glanced at us again. "No response to sodium bicarbonate for hemorrhagic shock. No response to epinephrine or even atropine to restart the heart. No response to blood and saline infusions. No response to cardiac massage."

Nevertheless, Rob continued cardiac compressions while I suctioned blood from his abdomen as he circulated fresh blood through the body manually, only to have it spill out in the abdomen again. With no visible results in ten minutes of CPR, Rob called a halt to the attempt.

He walked to the far side of the OR, head down, and removed his surgical gloves, throwing them in the metal trash can beside the OR table. After a brief pause, he looked over at me. "Sorry, Carl. We couldn't save this young man. We sure tried. We'd better go talk to the family if they're here."

I only nodded in affirmation. I didn't trust my voice to say a single thing as I removed my gloves and blood-saturated sterile surgical gown.

CHAPTER 12

When we returned to the ER to find and notify the family, Ann Kilgore saw by our expressions that the surgery had not gone well. "He didn't make it, did he?"

Still unable to speak, I shook my head.

After clearing his throat, Rob answered in a husky voice, "No, he didn't survive. Too much bleeding with terminal hemorrhagic shock. Do you know if the family is here yet?"

She nodded. "I just put them in the chapel down the hall. His young wife, Katy, is beside herself. Reverend White and her parents are with her." Her attention shifted to me. "I need you to see Michael soon. We've had several accidents this morning, and Dr. Neal hasn't had time to do anything but give him a brief exam and order blood work. If you can help us, he has lacerations that need sutured."

I nodded again and started to walk on when she stopped me a second time. "I almost forgot. At the scene, Robert gave Michael a message to give Katy. He doesn't know what it means but is very concerned that she get the message."

I finally found my voice. "Okay. I'll be back as soon as possible."

❧

THE SMALL CHAPEL with sky-blue walls and a soft-white ceiling just down the hallway featured an altar, a cross, and a Bible. The room was already crowded with family members when Rob and I entered. Reverend White had arrived only moments before us and stood beside Katy and her father, both seated near the front of the chapel. Katy's mother, seated nearby, gently rocked Mary Elizabeth in her arms. Four others, Robert's parents and two uncles, stood at the back of the room.

Clayton Harrison had his right arm wrapped around Katy as she leaned against him, tears streaming down her cheeks.

At seeing me, she stood. "Please tell me that Robert's okay. He's not hurt bad, is he?"

I looked down, searching for the right words, never an easy task when informing a family of the loss of a loved one.

Trembling and weeping, she nearly swooned as her father jumped up and caught her. "He's dead, isn't he? I can tell by the way you're acting." She began sobbing and hyperventilating as her father pulled her back down to his side on the small couch.

"I'm so very sorry, Katy. No, Robert didn't make it. The only comfort I can offer you is that he told me just a few weeks ago that he was ready to face any eventuality, including dying."

Robert's parents fell onto chairs, held one another, and sobbed.

Reverend White closed the door to the chapel for privacy as Katy began wailing, rocking back and forth beside her father on the couch. I did the only thing I could do at the time. I sat down across from Katy, bowed my head, and prayed silently for her comfort. No words would suffice at this time of loss and sorrow. Grief can only be shared by one's presence when words of comfort and solace are doomed to fall on deaf ears.

Clayton held his daughter close after the initial outburst passed.

Rob Hendrick took the opportunity to express his sorrow for the loss, reassuring the family that everything possible had been accomplished. He then excused himself, advising the family that he would be available for further discussion if desired.

Clayton looked up, nodded briefly, then gently rocked Katy back and forth beside him as she buried her head in her hands, weeping softly now.

Several minutes passed in shared silence broken only by the sound of weeping, as there were no dry eyes in the chapel. Katy's mom had collapsed into a rocker, still holding the baby. Reverend White stood with his hand on Katy's shoulder, his lips moving silently in prayer.

Finally, Katy mastered her emotions enough to speak. "Dr. Matlock, can you tell me why he talked to you about dying?"

I drew in a deep breath, slowly exhaled, and attempted to answer. "You know that Robert recently bought a lot of insurance for a young man without a lot of money and with a family."

Katy nodded.

"Robert pledged me to silence as long as he lived." I struggled with the lump in my throat, but finally continued, "He told me that he had dreamed about his funeral several times, always the same dream."

Katy dabbed at her eyes with tissues as fresh tears began to flow.

"There was a positive note to what he told me."

Clayton looked up at me with a frown on his face.

"I know that for those of us left behind, there is really nothing positive, but for Robert, he gave me quite a different ending to his story. He told me that each dream ended with an inexpressibly beautiful view of heaven as he heard the words, 'Well done, good and faithful servant.' Katy, your husband wasn't afraid of dying. He had looked into another world and decided that he had to make preparations for you and Mary Elizabeth to go on living."

Reverend White spoke up. "He didn't tell me about his dreams of dying, but I knew that he was very serious as I counseled and prayed with him in my office over the last few weeks. Robert did tell me that he no longer feared death, and we always concluded his visit with extended prayer for you, Katy, and for Mary Elizabeth." He paused and gazed around the room at every other person. "He also included all of you and numerous family members not present with us today. I trust that his prayers will not be in vain for those of you who don't know his Savior."

Silence ensued for several minutes as the family internalized what they had just heard.

Finally, I rose to excuse myself. "Katy, just so you know, another young man I take care of rescued your husband and was injured in the process. He's in the emergency room now, waiting on me to care for his injuries. He did say that he has a message to give you from Robert. He has no idea what it means but trusts that you will know."

Sniffing and drying fresh tears, Katy looked up at me. "I do want to know, but I'll just wait in here for a while. I don't think I could face anyone just now."

I opened the door to leave, but stopped as Katy called after me, "Can I see my husband, please?"

Robert's parents echoed their desire to view their son as well.

I closed the door once more and sat back down. "Yes, you and all the family may view him. First, however, I have to contact the coroner due to his traumatic death. We know the cause of death, but Art McKay has final say. In many cases, an autopsy is ordered."

Katy cringed at that unwanted news.

"But I'll find out right away," I assured her. "Since I know the cause of death and know Art so well, I'll see if he'll release the body. Legally, he does have final say at this point though."

IT WAS DEFINITELY GOING to be a long day. I hastened to the ER and first notified my office staff of the sad situation and that the morning would have to be rescheduled. Uncertain about the afternoon, I left that in limbo for the time being. A crushing pall of depression and grief settled on me after hearing Christine's partially restrained sobs as she acknowledged my message. It's never easy to lose a patient, especially one so young and well liked.

Dr. Neal approached as I sat at the ER desk after hanging up the phone. "Sorry I couldn't do more. I heard your first patient didn't make it. We had a number of MVAs this morning due to slick streets, heavy fog, and poor visibility. Most of the victims have only minor injuries from the crashes, but I still have four people to suture. I appreciate your helping with your other patient."

"That's okay, John. I know you did what you could in the short time before emergency surgery. He simply bled out from major abdominal lacerations. He also had a large cardiac contusion."

"That's what I figured was going on with him. Still, it's hard to lose one so young."

I nodded. "I'm going to see Michael Richards as soon as the coroner calls me back. Thanks again."

In less than five minutes, Ann Kilgore had Art McKay on the line and handed me the phone. "Hello, Art. This is Dr. Matlock. I don't know if you've heard about Robert Mills."

He responded in the negative.

"Robert was killed in a single-car accident this morning, crashing on the street here in Glen Falls. I understand he struck a fire hydrant and had to be pried out of the car by another one of my patients. We took Robert right to surgery, but he had multiple abdominal lacerations, the worst being of the liver and spleen. Dr. Hendrick even did open cardiac massage, but he also had a large cardiac contusion. He died mainly of hemorrhagic shock. The family is here and wants to view the body, but I need your permission first. I told them you might order an autopsy."

Art and I had a close working relationship, and he decided to forgo the autopsy since I was willing to sign the death certificate and had extensive knowledge of the cause of death due to the immediate surgery. None of the routine toxicologies ordered by Dr. Neal had revealed evidence of alcohol or substance abuse.

Relieved, I hung up the phone as Ann approached the desk. "Could you have the aides prepare Robert for viewing by the family? Art didn't order an autopsy since we know the cause of death."

She nodded. "Will do, but it'll be a while. Rather than taking him to the morgue, I'll have them put him back in one of our empty rooms for the family to view—that is, when we have an empty room. The place is still a mad house from all of these vehicle crashes. I'll send word to the family by one of my aides. They can continue to wait in the chapel. I sure hate what happened. Robert was a promising young man, always polite and hard working."

~

MICHAEL LAY QUIETLY on the cart in ER room 5, head and hands tightly wrapped in bandages to stop the bleeding. His wounds had been cleansed of grime and blood from the accident as he waited his turn for definitive treatment.

"Hello, Michael. Looks like you've had a rough morning," I said.

"You could sure say that, but how's the young man I pulled out of the wrecked car? I believe his name was Robert."

I shook my head. "Sorry to say, but he didn't make it."

Michael turned his head to the wall, not wanting me to see the tears trickling from his eyes. After several seconds, he reached up to blot his tears with the back of the bandage on his right hand. "Didn't mean to lose it. I've never been that close to an actual fatal accident before. He seemed a nice young man, and the death of my wife is still too fresh in my mind for me to handle this very well."

"I know. It has to be hard for you too. But you certainly did everything in your power to save him. I believe that's what caused your injuries, right?"

"Yeah, I guess so. But I just did what anyone else would have done to get him out of that wrecked car. It was about to catch fire and finally did."

"I'm not so sure that most people would have braved a developing vehicle fire to rescue a stranger, but you did. You've nothing to be ashamed of. You gave him a chance to live, if only his injuries hadn't been so severe."

The aide began removing his bandages. The blood was now mostly clotted and she scrubbed them after I injected sterile lidocaine for anesthesia. We worked rapidly, she prepping wounds and me suturing them. After about thirty minutes, I had sutured two occipital scalp wounds and one left-hand wound requiring closure. The singed eyebrow and hair on the left side of his face only required cleansing with sterile saline. The scrapes and abrasions of his hands, knees, and forehead were treated with topical bacitracin ointment.

Finally, I stood back and announced, "All finished, Michael. I've already reviewed your lab and X-ray reports ordered by Dr. Neal. No broken bones or serious blood loss, but you're going to be really sore for a couple of days or so."

"That's okay. At least I'm alive. One more thing. I need to give that young man's message to his wife. Is that possible?"

"She and the family are still here, waiting to view his body. I'll find out if she feels like seeing you. Meanwhile, I'm going to write some pain medication for you and release you from the ER. I believe you should go home and rest, so I'm recommending the day off today, tomorrow too if needed."

"Thanks, Doc, but no narcotics or anything habit forming. I don't want anything to make my head buzz after what I saw happen to my wife. I'm going to stick around and see if I can work. If Monty will let me, I believe I can do my job. I've got a minor headache, but my family needs the money."

I smiled. "Whatever you say, but I'll at least write your excuse if you decide you need to go home."

"Okay, but I won't use it unless Monty makes me go home."

"Wait in the ER waiting room when you get dressed. I'm going back to talk with the family now."

REVEREND WHITE, Katy, and her parents still waited in the chapel. Robert's parents had taken Mary Elizabeth to the cafeteria when they went for coffee, allowing Katy time alone with her minister and her parents. Other family members were directed to the cafeteria as they arrived.

Katy had cried until she had no more tears, only dry sobs, and she continued to sit with her dad's arm around her shoulders while her mother sat on the other side of her, holding her hand.

I entered quietly, not wanting to interfere as Katy talked softly with her parents. Between sobs, she asked, "What am I going to do? I have no job and no high school diploma. I have a sick, handicapped child and no resources in the world."

Clayton looked up when he noticed me waiting beside the doorway. "Doc, you said something about insurance, right?"

"Yes. Robert was approved for twenty-five thousand dollars of life insurance. Now that I think about it, he mentioned that it carried double indemnity for accidental death. If he was right, that means double that face amount."

Clayton squeezed her shoulders. "Honey, you do have some resources, and if you had nothing, your mother and I would gladly give whatever you and Mary Elizabeth have need of."

Katy shook her head. "I don't want twenty-five thousand dollars, or even ten times that much. I just want my husband back."

Clayton sighed. "I know, Katy. I know."

Bonita Harrison blotted her eyes with a tissue. "Do you know if there's going to be an autopsy?"

"It won't be necessary. Art said that I could just sign the death certificate. That's what I wanted to tell you. They're preparing Robert so you can see him in a little while. They'll bring him back down to the ER. I'll let you know when he's ready for viewing."

Clayton nodded. "Thanks for everything you and the surgeon did. We appreciate it, even though Robert didn't make it."

"There is one more thing I need to ask you. The young man who pulled Robert from the vehicle was the last person to hear him speak any coherent words. Robert told this young man his name and gave him a message for Katy."

Clayton looked at his daughter. "It's up to you, honey. Are you up to it now?"

"Yes, if Robert left a message, I want to hear it. Do you know this young man very well, Dr. Matlock? Is he reliable?"

"I know him quite well. He's also one of my patients. One thing you should know about him is that he just lost his wife before Christmas. He's trying to raise three small children alone. He works here at the hospital and is a good man. The sudden death of your husband has really hit him hard. He sustained several injuries trying to save him. I just finished repairing wounds and he has on several bandages. He looks very much the trauma victim also."

"Then I want to hear what he has to say, and I'm sorry for his loss too."

99

"Would you like me to bring him here so that you, Reverend White, and your parents can talk with him in privacy?"

Katy nodded. "Yes, please do. I want to thank him for doing what he could."

CHAPTER 13

*M*ichael waited in the hallway as I prepared the family to meet him. Opening the door, I motioned him into the chapel. He hobbled in the door and nodded. Looking up at him, they saw a serious young man, head swathed in a circular bandage above his ears, multiple bruises and abrasions of his face, and a singed left eyebrow from the flames. His left hand was covered with a bandage over the sutured area while the right had multiple superficial abrasions and contusions. His trousers were torn at the knees, and his boots were scuffed over the toes as a result of landing face down on the sidewalk.

I began the introductions. "Folks, I would like you to meet Michael Richardson. Michael, this is Katy and her mom and dad, Bonita and Clayton Harrison. This is Reverend White, their minister from Glen Oaks."

Michael nodded at each one in turn, then stepped forward to shake hands with Clayton and Reverend White.

"Thanks for what you tried to do," Katy said, "and I'm sorry that you were injured."

Michael hung his head. "I'm just sorry for what happened to your husband."

For several long seconds, no one said anything else.

Katy looked at him expectantly. "Dr. Matlock said you had a message from my husband."

"He did give me a message for you. I don't know what he meant, but he acted like you would understand. He said, 'Tell her I'm ready.'"

Clayton looked perplexed. "That's it? That's all he said?"

Katy burst into tears again. "Oh, Daddy, I know what he meant."

Michael shifted his feet self-consciously as Clayton tried to comfort Katy. "I'm sorry. I didn't know it would make things worse."

Katy soon regained control of her emotions and sat up, wiping away tears once more. "You didn't make things worse. You did exactly what Robert wanted you to do. I think Reverend White knows what the message meant. I know too."

Reverend White knelt beside her and took both of her hands. "I do know, Katy. Robert had several sessions with me in the last four weeks. His constant concern was not for himself, but for you, that you would be ready to meet the Lord if something happened to him. He told me more than once that he didn't want you to be bitter about Mary Elizabeth's handicap. His desire was that you make a full surrender of your life to the Lordship of Jesus Christ, but he never once told me about his dreams of dying and of heaven. I guess Doc Matlock was the only one who knew."

Katy sighed. "Ever since Christmas, Robert has been worrying me with talk of my bitterness and anger. He went so far as to question my sincerity as a Christian. He asked me every day, at least once, if I was ready for eternity. I had no idea that he had a premonition of death. I'm so sorry that I didn't listen to him. I should have been kinder, more understanding, but now it's too late." She put her head down and wept all over again.

Reverend White stood. "I think it would be good if we all had prayer for Katy, Mary Elizabeth, and the rest of the family. This is an especially difficult time for Katy, and I trust that she will do what her husband wanted and totally surrender to the will of God."

Katy trembled as she reached up to take Reverend White's hands again. "Please pray for me. Pray now. I will surrender to the will of God in memory of Robert and for his sake."

"That's good, Katy, but do it for Jesus' sake. That's what Robert really wanted."

She nodded and his prayer ascended to heaven on her behalf and on behalf of the family. When he finished, Reverend White shook Michael's hand. "Thank you, young man, for having the courage to help Robert in his time of need. You did more than you know. You took his dying wish for Katy seriously. Knowing Robert, I know he would thank you with all his heart if he could."

Michael looked down again. "I know what it is to lose a companion. My wife died just before Christmas." He choked up for a while before he could continue. "It's hard, very hard. I only wish I had as much hope as Katy has for her husband. I wish I knew that my wife pled for mercy at the last minute. She died after an overdose. I couldn't get her to quit doing drugs." Michael shivered, trying to stifle sobs that welled up from deep within his chest, while Katy and her family sat in stunned silence until he regained his composure.

Katy stood and gave him a brief hug as he stood stiffly, not quite knowing how to respond. "I'm so sorry for your loss too," she said. "This must be a very difficult time for you as well. You'll never know how much it means for me to know that someone cared for Robert in his hour of need. I appreciate that you had the courage to deliver Robert's last message to the family, the message of reassurance that he was ready to meet his Maker. That means everything to all of us."

"Well, I'd better be going," Michael said after a few moments. "If there's anything I can do for any of you, please let me know. I'm in Glen Oaks fairly often and would be glad to help. Doc's my family doctor too." With that, he turned and hurried out the door.

Katy sat back down between her parents, steeling herself for the moment of viewing, not really wanting to see Robert as he was, but also wanting to honor him one last time in private with her family at her side before leaving the hospital. I remained with them as we waited on word from Ann Kilgore that she had Robert ready for their viewing in the ER.

"Doc, is that young man all alone in the world now?" Clayton asked. "Does he have any other family?"

Certain that Michael wouldn't mind, I answered, "No, he's not alone. He has three children to raise, eight-year old Wendy, four-year old Howie, and nearly two-year-old Jimmy."

He shook his head. "That's tough too, Doc. Really tough."

"You're right about that, Clay," I agreed. "He's having a difficult time adjusting."

I ACCOMPANIED the family as they gathered to see Robert one last time in the hospital setting. The aides had sanitized his body, wiping away all signs of external blood and arranging his head on a pillow as if he merely slept, his body covered up to his neck with clean white sheets. His countenance appeared relaxed and at peace. Katy got through it better than I expected, then departed for home accompanied by her parents and Mary Elizabeth.

I finished rounds and finally got to the office at 2:00. We had decided on a start time of 2:30, planning to see only the emergencies for the day. Christine and Donna were in a somber mood the rest of the afternoon as they helped care for sick patients.

Word had gotten around town already, as it always does in small towns where everyone seems to either know or be related to everyone else. Those who visited the office did so with unusually subdued behavior, holding conversation to a minimum. Robert and Katy were well known and loved by the people of Glen Oaks.

The ladies and I were glad to unwind and sip coffee in the break room when the last patient departed and the doors had been locked for the day. Donna rarely drank coffee, but she joined Christine and me with her own cup as we sat quietly at the table.

"What are we going to do for the funeral?" Christine finally asked.

"I think we should close the office and attend the service," Donna said, then looked at me. "That is, if it's okay with you."

"It's certainly okay. My wife and I wouldn't want to let Katy down by missing the service for her Robert. She has a most-difficult road ahead of her. As to what we'll do in addition, I suggest we send a nice bouquet of flowers from the office and maybe a plaque or something for Katy to keep afterward."

"I think that's a good idea," Christine agreed. "I'm for it. Robert was doing such a good job caring for his family. I had no idea he was dreaming of his death when he came for the insurance physical. It certainly explains his actions in buying what had to be an expensive policy for the money he was making."

"Yes, he was a thoughtful, caring man. He really grew up when he married Katy and Mary Elizabeth came along. We'll all miss his cheerful face in town. How about you ladies picking out the flowers and plaque? The office will pay for half the bill, then we can divide the rest by one-third each. Does that sound fair?"

Donna smiled. "Sounds like you're paying more than your share."

"Not really. You both contribute to the income of the office by the work you do from day to day. If it sounds fair for you, it works for me."

Finally, the cups were drained of caffeine and the ladies departed for a floral shop open late in Glen Falls. I threw out the coffee grounds and noticed the sticker on the package we were using to brew coffee. The tag read, *Merry Christmas from your friends, Robert and Katy*. It was signed in Robert's normal scrawl.

VISITATION BEGAN Tuesday evening at Art McKay's funeral parlor. My wife and I waited in line, conversing quietly with friends and neighbors. Katy stood by the casket, speaking with visitors, accompanied by her parents and Robert's mother and father. Mary Elizabeth was cared for by a maternal aunt who stayed only a short time, then took the baby home with her.

We were nearing the head of the long line when my wife pointed out a small planter that had been placed near the casket. It looked somewhat out of place until I read the small attached card: *In sympathy, Michael Richardson and children.*

Art noticed us looking at it and came over. "I see that you found the planter from Michael. Katy requested that we put it near Robert, in a place of honor." He smiled. "His efforts to save Robert, a complete stranger at the time, while risking his own life, means a lot to both families. I hope he gets to attend the funeral. They would like him to be a pall bearer, but he doesn't have a vehicle of his own to come in."

"If he wants to come, I'll personally pick him up and take him home afterward," I offered.

"That's great. I'll let the family know that you'll bring him."

LATE THE NEXT MORNING, Reverend White officiated the funeral, preaching about how important it is to be ready, a chief concern of Robert prior to his death. Michael sat with me and my wife during the service. He no longer needed the bandages, and he had combed his brown hair neatly over the sutures on the back of his head. He was dressed in a new dark blue suit with a matching blue tie and highly polished black shoes. Despite his recent facial bruises and abrasions, his blue eyes and finely chiseled profile made for a handsome figure of a man.

At the conclusion of the service, he took his place with the other pall bearers just outside the main room while Katy said her last good-byes. I was startled to see Katy standing with Reverend White by the casket, just like Robert had described in his dreams, and glanced at the ceiling. Somewhere above, I felt Robert looking down with thanks-giving that Katy now could also say with him, "I'm ready."

Following a simple graveside service in the Glen Oaks Cemetery, Michael was invited by Clayton to partake of a meal with the family afterward. I saw him shake his head and look over at me, explaining that I was his transportation.

As I made my way over to join the conversation, Clayton said, "No problem. Doc and his wife are invited too. His office girls are staying, so he might as well."

"Okay with me. We'll take you home afterward."

Michael nodded. "I'll do whatever you want. I'm with you."

And so it was that Michael stayed and conversed with the Harrison family, particularly with Clayton, discussing the strange tragic events recently experienced by both families. After I let my wife off at home, I drove Michael back to Glen Falls. He had an excused absence to attend the funeral and had interestingly not taken off work for his injury at all.

We made small talk during the ride, but my curiosity was piqued. I finally said, "It looks like you and Clayton got along well. How do you like him?"

"I liked him just fine. He's a very nice man."

"Yes, he is that. Did he mention how Katy is doing?"

"He did some, but he also wanted to know how I'm getting along. I didn't know that people who were recently strangers could become so concerned about one another."

"Shared sorrows and tragedy can either bring people closer together or drive them farther apart. At least that's been my experience."

He considered that. "I'm sure you're right. He asked me to bring the children and have Sunday dinner with them later in the spring when things have settled down for Katy and the family."

I glanced at him as I pulled up to the hospital entrance. "Well, did you accept the invitation?"

Michael's face flushed a bright red for a brief moment. "I did. Do you think I did right by doing that?"

"Yes, I think it's okay. It's an appropriate interval from the funeral. I think you should go. You do want to, don't you, Michael?"

He hesitated only briefly. "Yes, if it's not too soon. There's something about Katy and her family. I really am attracted to them. They're good people."

"I totally agree. They are wonderful people."

He stepped out, closed the door, and waved as I pulled away from the curb. Now that was something I hadn't expected. An all-wise providence appeared to be taking a hand to bring healing after a double tragedy in the lives of two families. I felt a gentle spirit of peace and resolution following that time of great sorrow as I drove back to the office.

Christine and Donna would be delighted at what I'd just heard. I smiled to myself. I was as bad as those girls were when it came to spreading news about our patients in our little office circle of three! I could hardly wait to tell them.

CHAPTER 14

ichael Richardson and his children arrived early for the children's appointment on Monday, April 21, 1975. They were due for another round of immunizations, and Michael brought them in his newly purchased used 1970 Impala four-door sedan.

Wendy, now eight, wanted to be first. "I'm not afraid to get my shots. Daddy says I can have an ice cream cone at the drug store if I'm good."

Donna helped me as I examined each one prior to their injections. Michael stood by to assist in discipline if necessary. Howie, five years old and active, took a little more coercion in getting his vaccines, but one look at his father persuaded him to sit still. Two-year-old Jimmy was another story, but finally the exams were completed and Donna finished with the vaccinations.

I had a couple of minutes, so I stayed to talk with Michael while Donna took the children to the break room for suckers. "How is everything now? Your children seem to be adjusting fairly well."

"Better for sure, but they still miss their mother even though she neglected them the last eight or nine months of her life."

"How about you?"

"I still miss my wife, at least the woman I knew before she got hooked on drugs. I don't think I'll ever completely get over losing her. It's too bad that you didn't get to know her before substance abuse ruined her life. She was a lot of fun to be with and took good care of our kids. The drugs totally changed her personality."

Michael appeared uncomfortable, so I changed the subject. "Did you ever have dinner with the Harrisons?"

"No, but we're actually on our way to their house now. Clayton called and suggested that this evening would be a good time. He asked me to bring my family, so we're all here and ready. It'll be good for my kids to see how a normal family lives, at least I think it will be."

"Do you ever think about marrying again?"

"Sure, but I'd have to be certain. I really want my kids to have a mother in their lives. I don't really know how to raise a little girl. I'm afraid I'll make a tomboy out of Wendy. I can tell she needs a woman's touch already."

"What do you need to be sure about?"

"That the woman I marry will unconditionally love my children as I do."

"Yes, that's a critical factor in a second marriage when children are involved."

"Keep your fingers crossed for me. I'll admit to you that I'm interested in Katy Mills, but it's way too early for either one of us. I have no idea if she could ever be interested in a man with three children already, but I need someone to love and to help raise my children."

"So tonight is just an exploratory visit?"

"That's right. I just want them to meet my kids and see how everyone interacts."

"Especially Katy?"

"Yeah, Doc. Especially Katy."

I stood and shook Michael's hand. "Good luck, and may you and your family find happiness soon."

"Thanks. See you later."

~

THE NEXT DAY, I finished a little early in the office and was preparing to lock up after the ladies left when a car pulled into our lot. Glancing out the window, I saw Clayton Harrison get out of his vehicle and head for the entrance. I flipped the waiting-room light back on and opened the door. "Hello, Clayton. How're you this afternoon?"

"Fine, Doc. Looks like you finished a little early today. Hope I'm not interrupting any of your plans for the evening."

"Not at all. What can I do for you?"

He looked up at the ceiling, lost briefly in thought, then made eye contact with me. "How about a cup of coffee?"

"I'm sorry, but the coffee's all gone for the day."

"I didn't mean for you to serve me. I'd like for you to come to the drug store and have a cup with me, maybe talk a little and help me with decisions."

I smiled. "Could this have anything to do with your dinner guest last night?"

He looked down at his feet, then back up. "Can't fool you at all, can I?" He shook his head. "You're absolutely right. That's what I want to discuss with you."

"Clay, you know I can't give any medical information out."

"Doc, I don't want medical information. I want to know what you think of Michael Richardson. How about it? Are you coming?"

"Sure. I'll meet you there in five minutes."

He wiped his forehead with his right hand. "You had me worried there for a minute. I don't want to waste your time. I'm willing to pay you."

"That won't be necessary. Let's just do it."

SOON WE WERE SEATED at a booth separate from the main soda fountain and away from the rest of the diners at Barry House's establishment. Ethel, Barry's wife, made sure our coffee cups never ran out as she judiciously steered patrons away from us. I'm not sure what she knew, but not much escaped her attention in the small town of Glen Oaks.

"Doc, I want to thank you for taking time to talk with me. We appreciate everything you did for Robert, Katy, and the baby. Robert turned out to be much more of a man than I initially gave him credit for. His provision for insurance still amazes me. Katy ended up with fifty thousand dollars due to his death being accidental."

"Robert was an unusual young man. He really loved Katy and all of you. I'm still mourning his loss myself. But I know you didn't bring me here to talk about the past. None of that can be undone now."

He sighed and shook his head. "No, it can't be undone. What I'm concerned about now is the future. Katy moved back in with us, as you know. The baby is making progress, even getting some movement in her legs with therapy, but she'll never walk unless a miracle happens. But she's a bright little thing. We love her to pieces." He looked away, staring out the front window at the street as a pickup truck drove slowly past. Then he looked back at me after another sip of coffee. "I'm worried sick over Katy. She stays in her room most of the time. I often hear her sobbing when I walk past her door, which she keeps closed most of the time. She has little to say at mealtimes and eats very poorly. I know she's losing weight the way her clothes hang on her now. My wife is equally concerned. We just don't know what to do."

"A normal grief reaction over loss of a loved one can last for six months to a year. But this does sound more serious. If you can talk her into it, have her come see me in the office. Maybe I can help. Tell me, how did the visit with Michael and his children go?"

"Actually, very well. She seemed genuinely glad to see Michael and to meet his children. I think it was a link with her past, with Robert, if you know what I mean."

I nodded.

"After dinner, we all sat and talked in our living room. Michael has well-behaved kids for their ages, and he seems to be a swell person. I've never forgotten how he risked his own life to pull Robert from that burning wreck. That had to take courage, although he minimizes it."

"Was that the main topic of conversation?"

"No, not at all. We made a lot of small talk, and we talked about his new job. He seems very skilled as a maintenance engineer, does everything from electrical repairs to cabinet making. He didn't brag about it, just told us what he does. He's a likable and personable young man."

"You can be certain he's skillful. I understand his boss at the hospital has recommended him for chief of maintenance after his coming retirement, promoting him over several others, due to Michael's ability."

"I would like to know what you think of Michael as a person. He obviously needs a wife, with three small children to raise. What do you know about him?"

"I know he's a loving father. His children are well disciplined in the office. He recognizes his need for a feminine touch in raising his daughter and two sons. He attends church faithfully and has changed his life since the death of his wife. He was never involved in substance abuse himself. In short, I believe he's a fine young man, and he's lonely."

"So you're giving him a good character reference?"

"I certainly am. I admit that I've only known him for several months now, but he has impressed me as an honest and upright person."

Ethel waited discretely for a lull in our conversation, then stepped back to our booth. "Another fill up, gentlemen?"

"Yeah, you all make a fine cup of coffee," Clay said, holding his cup in both hands. "Nothing like a good cup of coffee. Would you like anything else, Doc? I'm paying."

"No, thanks. My wife will have dinner waiting for me at home."

Clay reached for his Cincinnati Reds ball cap. "Thanks for talking with me. It helps to bounce thoughts off someone else. Unless you see no reason that I shouldn't, I plan to call Michael and have him and the kids back in a couple of weeks. Sound good?"

"Sounds good to me, and whatever the outcome, I believe it'll do both Katy and Michael good to get away from their sorrows, if only momentarily. As you can imagine, Michael has no one to pour his heart out to anymore. It has to be hard, but he doesn't let it show."

We parted for the evening after Clay finished his final cup of coffee and settled the bill, and I drove away with a good feeling in my heart. Again I felt a higher providence at work in our small town. There's always hope and healing for hurting hearts and devastated lives.

CHAPTER 15

*W*ednesday, May 14, 1975, dawned with a brilliant sunrise as puffy cumulus clouds reflected soft-pink-and-rose mottling on the horizon. A refreshing balmy breeze ruffled my hair, and robins sang in celebration of life in tree branches above the hospital grounds as I pulled out of the doctors' parking lot after another busy night delivering a baby. Tired but refreshed by the sweet coolness of the morning air, I hurried home to shower and dress for another day in the office. The demands of private solo practice were many but the rewards inestimable in caring for wonderful people from my community.

Later in the office, the day progressed as usual with spring sore throats and colds, sprained ankles and abrasions sustained on the town's softball field, and worried mothers with questions about child rearing. I thoroughly enjoyed my job.

About midday, Christine rushed into the break room as I finished another chart. "Guess who's here?"

I looked up. "I'm sure I don't know, but I'll bet you're about to enlighten me."

"You know I am." Then pausing for effect, she bowed stiffly. "It's my pleasure to announce that Katy Mills has presented to this office for consultation."

I shook my head. "Christine, sometimes you're just too much."

She smiled sweetly. "I know. Aren't I wonderful?"

"What you really want me to ask about is the reason for the visit, correct?"

She bowed again. "You are so wise, oh, all-knowing physician."

"Oh, brother! This had better be good."

"I couldn't help but hear Katy talking to Donna about Michael Richardson."

"Now how could you possibly hear that unless you were eavesdropping just outside the exam room door?"

"Oh, wise one, you have found out the foibles of your loyal servant once again."

"Sounds more like your folly." I assumed a severe expression. "You know better than to spy on our patients."

"With great chagrin, but no remorse, I acknowledge my weakness to my kind employer. I can only plead for mercy now." She curtsied and folded her hands as if offering a prayer of supplication.

Chuckling aloud, I finally regained my voice. "Oh, get out of here, servant girl. Just don't disclose any office secrets."

"Not to worry, wise doctor. Christine knows all but tells nothing." She rushed from the room laughing as I stood to resume seeing patients.

Donna met me in the hallway. "What was that all about?"

"You know Christine, our very own drama queen. She can barely contain herself, building up a story of romance in regard to one of our patients."

She shook her head knowingly. "I've already dealt with Christine about her insatiable curiosity, but I'm afraid she's hopeless." She handed me the next chart. "This is the one Christine's dying to know all about. Katy's here to discuss her depression and her guilt."

"Guilt?"

"Yes, guilt. She'll tell you all about it. She's all set to see you."

I shook hands with Katy and sat down across from her, noting her deep-blue eyes, brunette hair, beautiful complexion, and sad, haunted appearance. If she realized that she was truly beautiful, she gave no outward sign of recognition. Reviewing her vital signs, I noted a ten-pound weight loss, and she had never been overweight. "How are you, Katy? Looks like you're losing weight."

She shrugged. "I'm not sure, but Daddy said I needed to speak with you. He said he talked to you a couple of weeks ago and that you might be able to help me."

"I'll certainly be glad to try. Why don't you tell me how you're feeling first."

"I hardly know where to begin, but you know most of my story already." She stopped to wipe away tears with her handkerchief. "I didn't know how much I really loved and depended on Robert until he was gone. I have a lot of guilt about the way I treated him toward the end. Oh, I wasn't mean or unfaithful, just constantly complaining about life's unfairness, our poor handicapped Mary Elizabeth, and on and on. I was very bitter at the time, not with Robert, but with God. Robert began preaching at me, asking me about being ready to meet the Lord. You know what his last message to me was, but I just shrugged it off, attributed it to him turning hyper-spiritual after the birth of our poor child."

"I do know, and it has to be hard. One thing I know about Robert, he loved and forgave you, if any forgiveness was needed. I'm not sure he felt you owed him any apologies. He was just concerned about you and the baby. That was the way he lived the last few weeks of his life. You know, he told me that he knew he had only a short time to live. That's why he took out the life insurance policy on himself. He wanted you and Mary Elizabeth to be provided for after what he correctly perceived as his impending death."

"That's a part of it, Dr. Matlock, but there's more. I haven't been a good mother recently. If Mom and Dad weren't helping, I don't know when Mary Elizabeth would be fed or changed. I've been totally preoccupied with missing Robert and feeling sorry for myself. I even stopped working on my GED. I must not be a good person."

"Now I know that's not true. I saw both you and Robert making great strides in personal growth over the last few months. You've been through more than any young woman your age should have to deal with. You're not yet quite eighteen, and none of this is easy, not at any age."

She looked at the floor, sighing deeply. "One other thing happened recently. When Michael Richardson came to visit, I enjoyed his company. But that doesn't feel right. It's not fair to Robert for me to enjoy male companionship. We weren't alone together, but even in the presence of all my family there seemed to be an unspoken bonding between us. Is that wrong for me to feel that way so soon?"

"No, it's not wrong," I assured her. "In fact, it's very natural. Both of you have suffered the loss of a companion, both of you have small children to raise, and both of you are quite lonely. I see no harm in your being friends now. After a few months of getting to know one another better, who knows? Perhaps there can be much more between you. I'm as certain as I can be that Robert would want you to find another provider for both you and the baby. He knew the money wouldn't last forever. It was only meant to be a temporary means of support."

"What should I do now?"

"The first thing to do is get out of your room. Become involved with all your family again, especially with Mary Elizabeth. Your dad tells me that she's making progress in therapy. She may never walk without some type of mechanical device, but she appears normal otherwise. She's gaining weight every time we check her on the scale here. She's going to need you intensely involved." I hesitated. "And she's going to need a father figure, not just your own dad. So developing friendship with a prospective partner isn't wrong. Just be sure to start out right with marriage vows first with Michael or whoever is Mr. Right for you."

She considered that. "So you think I should be getting back to normal now?"

"Whoa now, I didn't quite say that. In my experience and in many clinical studies, the average period of grief following the loss of a companion is six to twelve months. Even after that, you'll always feel a loss when you look at his empty chair, but time and God has a way of allowing our hearts to heal if we will reject bitterness and resolve to live life to the full."

Katy's expression became more peaceful. "I think you're saying that I need to start living as normally as possible under the circumstances, one day at a time, and not stress over the future. Is that right?"

"Yes, Katy, and God will give you the strength and grace for each day if you let him."

"Do you think I need to take medication for depression?"

"Well, depression and grief are not exactly the same thing. Grieving over a severe loss is normal. Too much of certain kinds of nerve medication has even been shown to extend the grieving process. Depression may or may not have a recognizable cause, and the treatment is different in most cases. Are you following me?"

"I think so." She managed a beautiful smile. "I need to do a lot of this myself."

"That's the way to start. But don't continue to shut out your family. Also, I know for a fact that your father thinks a lot of Michael. I believe he would be happy to see you and Michael as friends, and possibly someday as companions."

She took a deep breath. "It's a big order, but if Robert could face death with such equanimity, the least I can do is face life with determination."

"Exactly. And remember, your days will vary—some good, some bad—but the usual trajectory needs to be steadily upward. Take one small challenge at a time. The next one will be easier. You get the idea."

When she nodded, I added, "Make an appointment in two more weeks. Keep a diary of your feelings and your activity for each day. We'll review it next visit and decide if medication is needed or not. A deal?"

We both stood and she shook my hand. "It's a deal, Doc. I already feel a little better. One more thing. Should I go back to school in the summer session for my GED?"

"No, you've enough of an assignment for now. Think about putting that off until fall. You're young and have plenty of time. Don't make deadlines for yourself that you might not live up to."

"Okay. I'll see you in two weeks. Thanks again for your help. It means more to me than you'll ever know."

CHAPTER 16

*T*he summer of 1975 brought a lot of excitement to the office, with the birth of several babies in July and August along with the usual demands of our growing practice. Some days I seemed to be burning the candle at both ends, as the old saying goes, and there was no time for boredom.

Michael and his children were frequent visitors in Glen Oaks, and Christine kept Donna and me updated with the most recent gossip. Clayton Harrison and Michael Richardson developed a close relationship, becoming Saturday-morning fishing buddies even. And most evenings Michael and Katy could be seen strolling along Main Street, sometimes deep in conversation, other times just quietly enjoying one another's company.

Clayton and Bonita became regular babysitters for the Richardson children as well as for Mary Elizabeth during those warm summer evenings. To hear the town gossip, babysitting had been Clayton's idea. Some said that he and Bonita were really enjoying their new role as grandparents. Even ten-year-old Kenneth, Katy's brother, looked forward to Wendy and her siblings coming to play in the Harrison's spacious backyard. Of course there were others, gossips who claimed that Clayton had ulterior motives for babysitting. Some said he just wanted Michael for a son-in-law.

One morning, I drove down Main Street early on my way to work and saw Christine leaving Barry House's drug store. She arrived a few minutes after me. Donna was already at the office and had opened up to receive patients. No one was due to arrive for a few more minutes as Christine hurriedly made coffee.

Both ladies were busy with chores in the break room when I sat down to collect my thoughts and enjoy a cup of coffee before patients arrived. I looked at Christine and raised my eyebrows. "Having breakfast at Barry and Ethel's drug store these days?"

Christine flushed as Donna smirked. "She sure is. Want to know why?"

"Well, yeah. Did you forget how to cook?"

Christine shook her head.

"She's only there to gossip with all the other town busybodies."

Christine pushed her lips out in a pout. "That's not fair. Sure, we're discussing current events. You know. Nothing bad."

I frowned. "Current events?"

Donna wagged her finger at Christine. "In reality, the ongoing relationship between Katy and Michael has all the town biddies wagging their tongues."

"Oh, I see. Christine, have you joined the Glen Oaks gossip mill?"

Donna stood, arms folded across her chest, emphatically nodding her head.

Exasperated, Christine stuck out her tongue at her. "That's not fair. The food is good. I really enjoy visiting while sitting at the counter eating the delicious breakfasts prepared by Ethel House and her daughters."

"And taking part in the gossip. Admit it now."

"Okay, so you caught me. What's so bad about that?"

"I guess nothing as long as you remember to share no personal information from the office about either one of them," I said. "I don't want patients feeling that they can't trust us to keep silent about their health and personal affairs that we're privy to by necessity."

"Doc, I would never do that, so set your mind at ease." Christine laughed heartily. "My nose may be too long, but my mouth is sealed tight when it comes to personal details about our patients."

Donna laughed and left the room shaking her head.

Christine cleared her throat. "Besides, you'd be surprised how much everyone knows about Michael and Katy. There are no secrets in small-town USA. Isn't it wonderful? I just love it."

"Just be sure none of the secrets from this office are divulged by you. Okay?"

"Okay, chief. I'm pledged to silence in that regard."

Donna came back, bringing the morning newspaper that the delivery boy handed in the door.

Christine glanced at Donna, then continued to stare at me until I asked, "Is there anything else?"

"Why certainly, don't you want to know all the delicious news? It's about your patients. I would think you'd have enough interest in the people you care for to want follow-up. And don't let Donna fool you. She's dying to know too. She's just not brave enough to ferret out the information."

Donna made a face and muttered to herself.

"And you believe you have good information?"

"Doctor, you wouldn't believe the breakfast banter at House's drug store. It's not anything bad about them, just deliciously romantic tales of bliss."

"Christine, you're too much! But go ahead and tell me all about it. I have to admit to being exceedingly interested in a good outcome for those young folks."

Donna sighed. "Okay, you two. No one's in the outer office yet, and I want the best for them too. I just don't believe in prying into other people's business like a certain unnamed person working in this office does."

Christine looked at me. "See, I told you. She's just as interested as I am."

"Okay, go on."

"Well, Ethel House told me that they're now past the stage of simple friendship. She saw them holding hands twice last week."

"Is that your big news?" I asked. "Donna and I could probably come up with something better than that."

Christine looked hurt. "Well, I think it's romantic, anyway. We're still waiting for the news of the first kiss."

Donna looked shocked. "Christine, you're not spying on them, are you? That's not nice."

"Of course not, silly. How would I do that? Laura Dawson lives next door to the Harrisons. It's her job to report on what she sees in the moonlight when Katy and Michael sit on the front porch swing by themselves. She's part of our team." She looked momentarily downcast. "So far, nothing beyond sitting close and holding hands. Kid stuff!"

The bell over the front door sounded, alerting us to the entrance of the first patients. Donna sniffed and got up to see who had arrived. "Kid stuff indeed," she muttered. "Those gossips are worse than kids."

Christine smiled angelically before turning to go back to work. "See, I told you she'd like it."

"Just a second. I trust that you aren't creating the impression that our office is a hub for community gossip. That would certainly have an adverse impact on the practice. I don't like the idea of a gossip club meeting at the drug store, especially if Laura Dawson is involved in your conspiracy. Donna has a valid point about gossip."

Christine spun back around, laughing. "I'm just spoofing Donna. There's no gossip club. My stove top went out and I can't fix my usual breakfasts at home. So Ethel House is spoiling me with her tasty morning menu. What I said about Laura Dawson being a snoop is true enough. Everyone knows that anyway. Katy's the one who told me she noticed her standing in the dark watching them on the porch swing for over an hour. And Ethel House did mention how sweet it was to see them in a relationship that appears to have a healing effect on their lives. But rest assured, there's no club." She started to leave the room but turned around once more, resting her hand on the door knob. "Please, Doc, don't spoil it for me. Don't tell Donna about my little joke. After I get her really fired up today, I'll level with her before we leave tonight so she won't feel that she's working with a master spy."

"Okay. I won't spoil your prank, but don't carry it too far, please. I want Donna to be able to do her job." I chuckled as she left the break room. Christine sure livened up the place, and she had a heart of gold.

~

THE FOLLOWING SATURDAY MORNING, my wife and children were out of town visiting relatives, and on sudden inspiration, I decided to have breakfast at Barry and Ethel's drug store. The menu was always varied and delicious, making it the most popular place to have breakfast and lunch in the eastern part of the county.

I bought a newspaper from the vending box outside the drug store, tucked it under my arm, and entered to find a seat at a booth. Ethel House smiled and pointed to the booth farthest from the counter, knowing my desire to sit quietly and read the paper.

After ordering ham and eggs with buttered wheat toast and a large glass of milk, I began sipping my coffee and scanning the headlines. I was engrossed in news about county highway construction until Ethel brought my food. Glancing around, I saw Michael and Katy looking for a seat. The other booths had filled up, so I motioned them my way as I folded my paper and laid it on the seat beside me. "Good morning. You're welcome to have the seat across from me. It's pretty crowded this morning."

Michael waited while Katy scooted across to sit beside the window, then took the seat on the aisle. "Thanks, Doc. We appreciate it. Is your family out of town?"

"Yes, for the weekend. What are you two up to this fine morning?"

Katy smiled. "Michael's taking me canoeing. He'd better be a good swimmer because I'm not."

Michael grinned. "They'll have a life jacket for you to wear, and the stream's shallow anyway. We'll be fine."

"I'm glad to see you two enjoying life again. It's the best therapy in the world for both of you. How are the children?"

"Mary Elizabeth is growing like a weed," she said. "Michael arranged a day off to take us to Riley for her most recent appointment. I'm amazed at how she's taken to him. As long as he stood beside her, she let the doctors examine her without crying. She's never even done that for me. He has a way with children."

He shrugged. "It's nothing special on my part. She's just a sweet child."

"Katy's right, you do have a way with children. You needn't be so modest."

Michael cleared his throat. "My three are doing well. They love little Mary Elizabeth and compete for who gets to play with her first."

Katy nudged Michael. "Don't look now, but there's Laura Dawson. She hasn't seen us yet, but she will."

He grinned and reached for her left hand. "Let's give her something to talk about."

Katy blushed but took his hand as Michael called out and waved at Laura, making sure to have their clasped hands visible on the table top. "Michael loves to tease," she said to me. "Mrs. Dawson watches us on the porch swing. She turns her living room light off and stands in the dark thinking that we can't see her. It's really very funny. She's harmless, just nosy. She's lived next door to my folks for years, always wants to know what they're doing."

"Christine told me all about it. She even had Donna believing she was on a team with Laura to spy on you two. She finally told Donna she was joking."

It was good to see Katy smile and hear her laugh.

"I just love those girls who work for you. Christine is such a prankster, always laughing and having a good time. She's helped cheer me up more than once."

"I'm glad to hear you say that. Sometimes I worry that she's annoying people with her levity."

Michael shook his head. "No, not at all. She really brings a ray of sunshine to your office, and Donna brings a sense of acceptance and compassion. They're quite a pair. I wouldn't want them to be any other way."

I finished my breakfast and stood. "If you'll excuse me, I have a few patients to see in the office this morning. Enjoy your meal and have a great canoe ride. It sounds like fun."

Michael nodded. "Bye, Doc, and have a great day."

"And thanks for letting us interrupt your newspaper reading," Katy added.

That had been my pleasure. "I enjoyed your company. See you later."

CHAPTER 17

$\mathcal{J}$ had nearly completed early morning rounds at the hospital in early September when Michael approached me in the hallway of the main corridor. "Got a second, Doc?"

"Sure. What can I do for you?"

"I'd like your opinion. You know about my relationship with Katy and all the turmoil and sadness we've both had in our lives the last year."

"I'm sure life hasn't been easy for either one of you," I said.

He shook his head. "No, it hasn't, but the last few months, getting to know Katy and her family, have been the best days of my life. My children already love Katy."

"That looks to be true from the standpoint of an outside observer. What are you leading up to?"

Michael looked down, suddenly self-conscious. "Do you think it's too early for me to ask Katy to marry me? I mean, does it seem unseemly since neither one of our spouses have been dead for a year?"

I thought about that as Michael stood shuffling his feet. "I think you both have reason not to wait a long time. You and Katy both have young children needing the guidance and help of two loving parents. It would simplify both of your lives as I see it. You have to keep looking for babysitters, and she has a handicapped child who has really bonded with you. I'm sure most people will understand.

Anyway, if you love one another, who cares what anyone might think?"

He sighed. "I was hoping you would say something like that. I appreciate you and value your opinion."

"Michael, you're doing a good job with your family, but you could sure use help. I believe Katy would be a great asset, especially in raising Wendy. She would also fulfill a valuable role in the lives of your little boys. They need a mother too. I think it's great."

"Thanks a lot."

"You're welcome. So when are you going to pop the question?"

"This evening. Say a little prayer for me. I'm pretty nervous about her answer. I don't want to rush her if she isn't ready. I don't want anything to cause a break-up."

"Katy is a level-headed young woman. Whatever she says, I don't think she'll want to break up. I've seen the way she looks at you. I'll keep my fingers crossed. I believe it's the logical next step if you truly love one another."

Departing for the office, I knew the ladies would be more than excited. Over the last several days, they had talked of little else during any brief downtime between tasks.

DONNA WAS in the break room when I arrived, and I hung up my jacket before saying anything. "Is Christine busy?"

"The phone is already ringing nonstop. Every time she gets off the line with a patient, another one rings in. It looks like September cold-and-flu season blew in with the start of the school year as usual."

"If you would like to hear it, I have news about Michael and Katy. You can tease and entice Christine today as long as you want before you bring her up to speed."

"I'd love it. She needs a comeuppance."

I'd thought so. "Michael plans to propose to Katy this evening. I think it'll go well, but we'll soon know."

Donna clapped her hands. "That's wonderful. Now don't tell

Christine, no matter how much she badgers you, and she will. I'll tell her the full story when it's time to go home."

"Don't worry. My lips are sealed. It's time you had a little revenge."

"It sure is, and how sweet it'll be!"

～

BY THE END of the day, Christine was frantic for the information. The patients had all been seen and dismissed, and Donna still hadn't divulged her special knowledge. I moseyed into the waiting room just to listen to their banter.

Christine finished closing the books for the day and jumped up from her desk. "It's just not fair. I haven't been able to concentrate all day long. I saw Michael drive down Main Street an hour ago. He must have got off work early. What's going on? Someone please tell me." Then she collapsed back onto her chair.

Donna glanced at me. "Doc, you think she's had enough?"

"I believe so. You can tell her whenever you want."

Donna leaned down and whispered in Christine's ear.

Christine's expression was priceless as she leaped up and yelled like a cheerleader for a last-second winning shot at the state basketball game. "Yippee ki-yay! Wonderful, wonderful!" She whirled about in a circle, rushed to grab her jacket and scarf off the hook, and ran for the door.

Donna stepped out of the way. "Have you lost your mind? Where are you headed?"

"To the drug store, of course. The source of all intel. See you."

I laughed until Donna pointed out the window. "Look who's coming. Christine no sooner drove out of the lot than another car pulled in from the other direction."

Michael opened the passenger door for Katy and helped her out. She looked up at him with a beautiful smile and took his arm as he escorted her to the front door.

Donna hurried to open it for them. "Hello, Michael, Katy. What a surprise." She closed the door behind the happy, smiling couple.

Katy looked around. "Where's Christine? We hoped to see her too."

Donna laughed. "She rushed to the drug store hoping for information. She saw Michael drive into town earlier than usual, and you know Christine."

"I'm sorry she isn't here," Michael said, "but we wanted you to be first to know that we're engaged."

I shook Michael's hand while Donna hugged Katy. "We're all very happy for you. I'm including Christine. She just left a little too soon. I've told her that her curiosity would be her undoing. Donna has been teasing her all day."

Donna evidently felt a little guilty about teasing Christine mercilessly, for she had a sudden inspiration. "Have you got a minute?"

When they nodded, she said, "Let me call the drug store and have her come back. I think I can guarantee that she'll be here in record time."

Within a mere two minutes, Christine's car slid into the parking lot, throwing gravel and screeching to a halt. She was out of it almost before it was fully stopped. She ran to the door and burst into the office, nearly breathless. Hurrying to Katy to hug her tight, she exclaimed, "It has to be good news."

Katy nodded.

"Hooray!" She went on more calmly, "I've been praying for this. You're both my favorite people."

Donna stiffened. "Well, where do I fit in?"

Christine pulled Donna into a group hug with Katy. "Oh, you know what I mean. You're all my favorite people." She paused, glancing my way. "Doc too."

I looked at Michael. "When's the big day?"

He looked at Katy.

"Wednesday, December twenty-fourth," she said. "I want a Christmas Eve wedding. I suspected Michael was going to ask me soon. I already had the day picked out."

I nudged Michael. "And you were worried about asking."

He grinned. "Yeah, I know. Well, we don't want to hold you up. We're on our way to tell her parents. I talked to Clayton and had his blessing a couple of weeks ago. He probably thinks I chickened out. I guess I did have to get myself together. I didn't know what she would say."

I clapped him on the back. "We're very happy for you, as you can see."

Michael and Katy left the office hand in hand, smiling and so happy.

Christine grabbed Donna by the arm. "Well, come on. We've got to start making plans for the celebration."

Donna stared at her. "Where are you dragging me now? It's their wedding to plan, not ours."

Christine only pulled more forcefully. "We're going to the drug store to celebrate with a chocolate soda. I'm treating. And we do have to decide on tin cans and streamers to tie to their car after the wedding. Lots of good stuff like that."

Donna called back over her shoulder as Christine urged her on, "She's hopeless. I'm just going along to make sure she doesn't hurt herself."

It was a delightful ending to the day—a day filled with promise and anticipation.

EPILOGUE

*C*hristmas Eve, December 24, 1975, finally arrived. Donna and Christine had been given the responsibility of planning much of the wedding for Katy, with Donna acting as wedding coordinator and Christine being her assistant. The excitement level in the office leading up to the Christmas holiday had been almost overwhelming with the ladies constantly planning, patients bringing in holiday treats, and the normal bustle of the season.

Katy and Michael were a lovely couple as they stood at the front of the Glen Oaks Community Church, repeating their vows, as Reverend White officiated the ceremony. Since both had previously been married, Michael wore a black suit with a long dark blue tie and Katy wore a blue velvet dress with a white hat and simple veil. Most of the adult population of Glen Oaks and many from Glen Falls attended the ceremony. The little church was packed as friends and family gathered to wish this young couple good luck.

The Harrisons sat in the front row holding Mary Elizabeth and Jimmy. Wendy and Howie sat with Katy's younger brother, Kenneth, beside the Harrison family.

Christine stood at the back, greeting guests and making sure everyone signed the guest register. Donna scurried here and there, making sure that all the last-minute details were taken care of.

Two of Katy's cousins served as ushers and seated my wife and me across from the Harrisons on Michael's side since he had no close family to attend the wedding. Jan Hart—hospital aide, good friend, and frequent babysitter for Michael's children—sat beside my wife. Michael's friend Wyatt was his best man while one of Katy's older cousins served as maid of honor.

It was a simple ceremony, and the young couple were soon on their way to the reception at the church recreation hall next door. When the festivities were completed, Michael and Katy hugged the children, then ran through the blizzard of rice showered on them while a blast of icy wind and swirling snowflakes pelted them as well.

As they drove off, five long strings of tin cans clanked noisily on the road behind them. Christine had completed the last of her duties with a flare. The young couple were off to a secret honeymoon destination, only to be disclosed upon their return to Glen Oaks, where they would reside in a four-bedroom house on Main Street. Amazingly enough, Christine had completed all the reservations for them and kept their itinerary secret from everyone, even Donna.

The community came together in support of this lovely young couple who had suffered such severe loss in the recent past. Glen Oaks was a family community with a big heart for those experiencing misfortune.

IN THE SPRING OF 1976, Michael and Katy announced the expected birth of a child after confirming the diagnosis with me in the office. But their biggest surprise came when they announced plans to adopt a handicapped child in the coming weeks. Another infant girl, two-month-old baby Ruth Marie with cerebral palsy and unwanted by the birth parents, would formally soon be a part of the growing Richardson clan.

And so it happened that the family quickly expanded to eight when Robert Mills Richardson arrived on the scene in the fall. It became a familiar sight in the spring of 1977 to see Michael pushing a stroller for two with both infants enjoying the ride. The older children skipped and walked merrily along while Katy pushed Mary Elizabeth in a special cart made just for her. The family became an inspiration to the entire community.

$\sim$

TIME SEEMS to pass far too quickly for most of us as we grow older. The people of Glen Oaks seemed to take the Richardson family for granted after a year or two. But Michael and Katy continued to have a special place in my heart as a wonderful example of the resilience and generosity of the human spirit. That was especially true when I drove by the Glen Oaks Cemetery on May 30, 1977.

I noticed Michael and Katy surrounded by their children decorating graves and stopped to say hello. I pulled up and parked my car nearby. "It looks like you have the entire crew here today, Michael," I greeted him. "How are you?"

Coming toward me, Michael held out his hand. "Just great. It's good to see you."

Katy knelt at a gravesite she had just decorated with a floral arrangement. "Come see the decoration, Doc. I think you'll like it."

I made my way across fresh-cut lawn to the monument and noticed the engraving: *Robert Mills, Beloved Husband and Father, Taken Too Soon, But Ready For Eternity*. Michael stood with his arm around Katy's waist as they admired her handiwork.

It took me a while to find my voice. "So beautiful and appropriate. He certainly became a man of faith. He was ready for eternity for sure."

Michael nodded. "I'm doing my best to care for the beautiful child and wife he left behind."

We stood in silent contemplation as a gentle breeze fluttered the decorations throughout the cemetery. I glanced at an Army veteran's grave nearby, the small US flag proudly waving in the wind. I turned to walk with them back to the vehicles, with Michael carrying both handicapped children in his arms. "You know, Robert was never in the military, but he became a proud soldier of the cross and a defender of the family."

Michael nodded and I noticed tears in Katy's eyes. She finally spoke up. "The reason we were able to adopt Ruth Marie was due to the insurance settlement after his death. "We adopted her in his honor, and now we're off to decorate Marilyn Richardson's grave in Glen Falls."

Michael's eyes teared up as he turned to me. "I don't know if she was ready or not, but she was the mother of three of our children. We plan to honor her memory. Katy and I don't want the children to ever forget their roots or lose respect for those who helped establish our little family."

They were about to drive off when I hailed them.

Michael rolled his window down.

"What's this I hear about a new charitable foundation?" I asked.

He smiled. "The money Robert left is growing, and we don't need it all. We decided to take five thousand dollars and start a charitable fund for handicapped children. We're hoping to put collection jars in all the offices in Glen Oaks. God has been so good to us, and that's why we decided to adopt Ruth Marie. We want her to have a chance in life, and we want to bring assistance to other handicapped children as we honor Robert's memory."

Briefly overwhelmed at the maturity and love demonstrated in this family, I could only say, "Bring a collection jar to our office. We'll be glad to contribute and help with the donations."

Katy smiled and waved as they drove away.

As I watched them ride out of sight, I recalled a portion of a verse from Song of Solomon, chapter 2: "My beloved is mine and I am his." The next verse beautifully adds, "Until the day break, and the shadows flee away."

It was with deep gratitude that I realized the shadows had flown away from this family, banished from their lives by love for one another, love for others, and love for the Lord. The spirit of Christmas lived daily in their lives of giving and sacrifice as triumph overcame tragedy.

ALSO BY CARL MATLOCK MD

Book 1 The Annals of A Country Doctor

Book 2 Reminiscence: Life of A Country Doctor

Book 3 Rebels, Romans, and the Rabbi

Book 4 Jerusalem Crucible

Thank you so much for reading. Reviews on amazon.com are welcomed and appreciated.

I can be reached at DoctorCarl@carlmatlockmd.com.

My website is https://www.carlmatlockmd.com.

I can also be reached on Facebook at Carl Matlock MD / Author.

Made in the USA
Lexington, KY
22 December 2019

58855112R10079